⌘

Agapi Mou

⌘

[my beloved]

Donnie

Travel with care
eyes wide open
yaseen!
Dynnee 14/6/14

Works by Donald I Horn aka Donnie

Plays

After The Rain
'...tell Mama, good-bye...' [published by Rain City Press – Seattle WA]
Don't know the colour of rainbows, actually
Dishin' With Divine [published by Rain City Press – Seattle WA]
Too Many Pennies and not enough Dimes
Milk the Cow

Musicals

Tonya and Nancy: The Rock Opera   adapted by Donald Horn and Elizabeth Searle from the Opera: Tonya and Nancy [musical about Tonya Harding and Nancy Kerrigan]
Night With Day [the life and times of Billie Holiday]
'69 – the sexual revolution musical   book by Donnie (Donald I Horn)
J.C. (HIStory) The Gospel According to an Angel

Books

Crumbs of Love [and that's all you'll ever get] [published by I Universe Press Chicago IL]
Agapi, Mou [my beloved]

Upcoming Projects

Tonya Harding: Me
Crumbs from the table of Love [sequel to Crumbs of Love]
How do you say murder in Greek?

⌘ Agapi Mou ⌘

[my beloved]

Donnie

Based upon true facts, this fictional novel is about one family and lost love. Various stories are woven together such as a box left to a granddaughter containing a necklace and a manuscript; an unexpected trip to an island of Greece and past events that has and will change all their lives.

This is a work of fiction. Names, characters, places and incidents either are the product of the author's imagination or are used fictitiously. Any resemblance to actual persons, living or dead, events, or locales are entirely coincidental.

Copyright © 2009 by Donald I Horn aka Donnie
All rights reserved

This book is for the residents of Zakynthos Greece
With a special dedication to Ellyn Bye.

⌘ Denny ⌘

I tried as gently as I could to close the door. She's resting now, it's been a long couple days.

Creeping down the hall, I noticed a light under the door of my mother's room. Should I knock? No, the hour was late and well, what words could be spoken? Besides, I had something I needed to do.

Earlier that evening Nana had pressed an envelope into my hand. Her voice was shaky but clear, 'Read it tonight my dear. And, read it alone.' I nodded, then bent over and kissed her forehead. She smiled, closing her eyes to me and the world.

She had been restless, so Dr. Windorf came by to check up on her and a decision was made to give her a couple of sleeping pills, 'They'll make her more comfortable.' he said.

'That's all we ask.' my mother replied, 'isn't that what any of us want?'

He smiled, 'I'll be back in the morning.'

With that, she walked him out and had gone to bed herself.

All of this had occurred around eight and here it was, looking down at my watch, 'past midnight?' I need to get some rest myself. Standing, I felt that I had sat longer than I should have and my joints were stiff. Walking over to the bed, I leaned over and pulled

Nana's favorite comforter; a rose pattern, tattered on the ends and thread bare, to her chin. My thoughts immediately went to when I was little, and she used to let me crawl up into her lap and wrap both of us in it, squeezing us tight and making me giggle. 'How I wish I could do that for you now.' Bending further, I kissed her cheeks. Both sides, that is what I had always done, right Nana? *'It is polite to kiss on both sides of the face especially when you are acknowledging older people. It shows respect.'* As I grew older, she was the only one that this was done for, the one person that I had the most respect for. Gently touching her cheek and I whispered, 'you are not the only one getting old. I'll see you in the morning.'

    As I pulled back my hand, I noticed a single hair that lay loose against her skin so, ever so gently I placed it back with the rest of the grey hair which was neatly combed back from her forehead. My eyes moved to her sharp nose that centered her face, the eyelashes, oh those wonderful eyelashes that curled ever so and those lips, the ones that spoke wisdom and gave me love. Gently, I touched them, 'I love you.'

    Quietly, I closed the door, but as so many times before, just as the door closed, there was a click.

Slowly making my way down the hall, a slight twinge went through my body, which almost made me a giggle. Wasn't this like the old days? Getting home late from a date, sneaking to get past Nana's door and now this one? Both closed, and both containing the two women that loved me the most.

Tip toeing down the long hallway I looked at the worn wool diamond patterned rug under my feet. Nana and I would play hop scotch when it was too cold or rainy to play outside. 'We won't tell your mother, she wouldn't like it very much.'

After my turn, I would say, 'Your turn Nana.'

She would look at me, take a deep breath. 'Here goes nothing.' Something she always said, like it was her first. She would hop and skip down the hallway, laughing then lean up against the wall and say, 'Oh my, that's a long way for an old lady.' We continued to do it until we heard the car door shut or the phone ring and we'd run into her room, lie on the bed and laugh. 'My, what fun.'

At my door, I turned, and looked down the hallway. In the dim light I saw what I had always known; the old runner, photos, some of family hanging neatly on both walls, some collected from what seemed like centuries; picture frames of all shapes and sizes.

Closing my eyes, I could hear Nana's voice which seemed as clear as if she was standing right next to me said, *'Remember dear, sometimes memories are better than gold or any riches. No one has lived them except you. Aren't we lucky?'* Out of my being came a sigh, we certainly are.

Once reaching my door and the handle, I was struck by just how much commotion had filled this house, more so in the past few weeks than had in many years. Doctors and nurses coming and going as well as family members, some I hadn't even met making their way up and down the stairs, into this hallway and then into Nana's room.

But now, quiet.

As I pushed through the door, it creaked as I slid into the darkness.

Finding my way to the edge of the bed, I switched the bedside lamp on, pulled back the covers, crawled into the only bed I had ever known, plumped up the pillows and reached into my pocket. The crumpling of the envelope was the only noise I heard. Once again, I heard Nana's voice, *'Read it tonight, my dear, and read it alone.'*

But why? What was the urgency?

I pulled back the flap of the envelope and found a small note.

Dearest one-
Forgive my writing. Time is near. Forgive me for leaving you.
Read my diaries, they will tell you it all.
Lovingly,
Nana

Flipping the note over, nothing. Reading it a second, then a third time, I felt cheated...that's it? Folding the note up and putting it in the envelope, the days toll crept into my body; helping comfort Nana...working with the doctor and nurses exhaustion was seeming into my being. So I placed the envelope on the night stand and switched off the light. Sleep came easily and swiftly.

⌘

A jolt ran through my body and I sat straight up and yelled. 'NANA!'

Pulling the back the covers, I leaped out of bed and right into my mother.

'I'm sorry dear.' She stood still.

I looked up at her face, where there had been pink cheeks and a sparkle in her eyes, now all I saw was the look of grief. Her beautiful blue eyes were now blood shot. 'She's gone.'

My body melted right into hers, 'She's gone?'

'I'm afraid so.'

I hugged her for what seemed like hours not wanting to let go.

Finally, she pulled back, 'She's been taken down to the ambulance and I'll be riding along with them.' Her composure almost failed her, 'the doctor promised that he would get me home.'

I moved past her, down the hallway and into the room where I had left Nana sleeping not so many hours ago, walking slowly to the bed. 'Nana? Nana?' My knees gave out and I was sobbing into a bare mattress.

A hand touched my shoulder. 'She went in the night as we all slept. She loved you very much. And,' her voice cracked as her hand left my shoulder. 'I need to leave now.'

I stayed buried in the mattress as the footsteps left the room, down the stairs. A loud sound shook the house as the front door tightly closed, then there was nothing but quiet.

Grabbing the comforter I dragged it over to the rocking chair began rocking, back and forth; back and forth. The stillness was broken with the back and forth motion of the rocking chair on the hard wood floor.

Not knowing how long I had been there...I was startled by the sound of the door opening, 'Mom?'

'Yes dear, it's me. I knew I would find you in here.' She came over and sat on the ottoman which we had given to Nana some years ago. '*Gotta keep my feet up the doctor says, what do they know anyway?*'

I reached down, 'Long day.'

'You know, she was a great woman. I'm glad she was mine for the time I got to spend with her.' She stretched her back and then placed her hands together on her knees, 'it had to happen, I knew it but...'

Curling into her I felt her body shake, 'it's just us two now.'

'Lucky you.'

I don't know if I felt a laughter or what, but she pulled away and started wiping her face, 'You know she, um, left you that box of things over there. She was my mother, but she always had something special with you. More than...' her voice trailed off.

I closed my eyes. 'She was the best Nana I could have ever wished for.' I let the comforter fall as I left the rocker and crossed over to the table where a large box lay waiting for its contents to be shared.

'You'll find some, diaries in there and oh, even a portion of a book she was writing.'

'Have you ever...'

'Read any of the stuff in there? No, that was hers and I just felt that she wasn't ready to share it yet.' She stood and walked behind me, 'that's all meant for you now, something she knew you would like. Given to you with all her love.'

I leaned into her arms, 'She is really gone.'

⌘

Lifting the lid, I noticed a note at the top, scribbled in the same hard to read writing that my note was written in.

Let the service be small. I know that tradition would have it that I be buried, but I want, if you would, that I be cremated. But lay my ashes next to my husband.

Flipping over the paper, nothing. Just like the other.

Mom commented, 'What we do for our men.'

'She loved him dearly.'

'That she did. Your Grandfather was a great guy – too bad they didn't get to live their lives out together.'

Looking over I saw tears well up in her eyes. I put my arm around her shoulder but my voice, the voice of reason, of comfort wouldn't speak. The pain of that night, even twenty years later seemed to be still fresh. I knew that she was thinking about her own husband, my dad.

It was my high school graduation, the excitement in the house that night could have filled a ballroom of party goers on New Year's Eve. Dad said he was going to be late, but that none of us was to drive, that was his job. Being a tax attorney and partner at a local law firm brought great demands on him even though tax season had ended, but he wanted to drive his family to the final even of his baby girl turning into a woman.

But as he drove home, he was broadsided by an oncoming car that had run a red light. When the phone rang, Nana knew. She turned, 'It isn't good.'

For years it was the three of us, Nana, Mom and I; the Three Musketeers. Now, just two left.

'Coffee?' Broke the silence.

'That, and some orange juice.'

'All right.' Trying to busy herself she leaned over kissing me on the forehead and left the room in a hurry.

I slipped the paper back into the box. 'I'll be back,' and followed Mom down the stairs.

Entering the kitchen I saw someone who didn't want to stop. She took out the two glasses, the carton from the refrigerator and began to pour while chatting away. 'I'll call and arrange a simple service. Seems that having her cremated (her voice waivered)'. After placing the glasses filled with orange juice she went right over and began pour us cups of coffee.

'Mom, that's what she wanted.'

'Here,' placing the mug in front of me, 'it's pretty hot.' Then she reached over the counter for my hands, 'It's going to be very hard to get used to. She's been here for well over thirty years in this house...'

I couldn't help but look into her eyes, 'practically all my life.'

Drawing back she lifted her mug toward me, 'Don't know if there is such a thing as the Two Musketeers, but here's to the two of us.'

'Here, here.' We said together, but after clinking our mugs together, an awkward silence settled in.

Then, what seemed to be out of nowhere, she asked, 'Honey, this kind of changes your plans, right?'

I almost spit out my coffee, 'Plans? I hadn't thought. Well, I took a sabbatical to help out with Nana— then summer – I'll probably go back to teaching in the fall. Honestly, I don't know.'

I took the glass with orange colored substance and began to swirl its contents.

'I think I'd like to sell this place.'

I nearly dropped the glass, but instead spilled it on the counter. Yes, I had waited for her to say these words since dad died. But I wasn't as prepared as I had thought.

She grabbed a paper towel and started wiping up my mess. 'It shocks me too to think like this.' That's when the tears began to flow.

I led her to the couch, where after finding a couple night time sleep pills and a throw cover she slipped into a fit full sleep.

Standing up I leaned backwards to stretch, then looked around the room, 'Maybe it *is* time.'

⌘

My body seemed to take its time up the staircase. Whew, maybe I should take one of those sleep pills myself. Entering the room startled me for a second. For months Nana had lain in the bed, or by the window, greeting me with her warm voice. But not now, the bed was bare, stripped of all that had been. A cold chill crept in as I made my way over to the box.

Back again, I see.

Turning, I expected to see Nana in the chair, smiling and encouraging me on to share her things.

'Nana?'

No, the room was empty except for me. No sooner had I picked up the box than I found myself on the bed bringing it into my lap. Did I have the courage? Taking a deep breath, I lifted my head and said, 'Well, here goes.'

I could hear her, *Oh, you'll like them, these personal things of mine.*

Looking down, I couldn't help but ask, 'Will I find some terrible truths? Lost stories? Family secrets?'

Curiosity has got the cat! Why yes, all families have secrets. They shouldn't be secrets now. You my dear are the last of the secret keepers of this family… since I am gone, they can be told. You will finish the story I began and I know you will tell all of them well.

The flaps pulled back easily, and the treasures that Nana held deep to herself were there. I began lifting out typed pages of what looked like a beginning of a manuscript, several diaries, a silver chain…what does all of this mean? Further down a map of Europe and a travel book of Turkey and Greece. And a note.

Dearest –

I see you have begun the journey. All the pieces of the puzzle are here, except an airplane ticket and some money. You will have those also. Travel well and finish my work.

Lovingly,
Nana

⌘

I carefully placed everything in the box as I had found it, except for the typed pages. Flipping through I found the type familiar, all typed on the old Olivetti that sat on the desk next to the window.

I never will get used to a computer. I like the feel of the key strokes. It makes me feel like I have written each word. Like a piano, the sound of keys coming together to make a symphony. Glorious!

The first page just said, *The Flower of the Levant.* What in the hell does that mean? Flipping to the next page, 'I guess we shall soon find out.'
Chapter 1

No one truly knows my island, my people. I feel that I must tell you these things so as to ensure that they are told correctly, that the information you receive is correct, or as correct as I can give them. It has been home for generations past of my family or should I say my papus' family. Our home, our way of life, our Zakynthos. Some have called it Zante, because of the Venetians, but it will always be the lovely Greek island of Zakynthos to me.

'My grandmother is from Greece? Okay, Nana...what lunacy have you begun?'

Where you may ask is this? Ah, it is located in the Ionian Sea, next to Kephalonia and six islands south of Corfu. From the east you can see the mainland of Greece – the shipping port of Kellini which at night, the lights shine bright as a beacon to tell us that we are not alone; and if you were to climb over the hills to the west, on a clear day you are able to see the coast line of Italy. And there, I must tell you are many clear days here.

This place, my island, has been ruled by many – first Troy where our lovely name has been given; ZA means 'a lot', Kynthos means 'hill', and others say it means 'a lot of hills and fruit'. We are also proud to say that we were even mentioned in the Iliad of Homer! Yes, for a Greek, this means we have a great place in history and not just because of war, politics or our fruit.

We have seen the Trojan Wars; thereafter Spain ruled for awhile, then we endured the Persian Wars, The Peloponnesian Wars, and even Rome came and conquered us!

Some claim that Mary Magdalene coming from Jerusalem on her way to Rome and then onto Spain and France stayed for about one year, in the year of our

Lord 34. The village of Martez (or Maries) some say was founded by her. We then are blessed to have had such a holy woman – who knew our Lord and was guided to stay on our small island.

'Nana, this sounds so Da Vinci Code! It can't be true.'

Terrible times were endured during the Byzantine Period as the pirates and barbarians raided our homes and fields. During this time, treaties were signed and the Turks were to rule Kephalonia and the Venetians, Zakynthos. It was to our relief that the Venetians came and even though they conquered us, it was actually they who rescued us. They organized our capitol – constructed the citadel and even our port was expanded and greatly developed.

With their coming and all the good they brought – commerce, infrastructure and peace; they also brought something called Nobles. The Nobles. Yes. Actually, division. Our populace was divided into three sectors; The Nobles; these were the ruling class voted into power by each other as they were both rich and they were the upper class of society. Their names were placed in the Golden Book (Libro d'oro) and only those who bore a title of nobility were allowed to have their names written there. The second class of people were the Asti or civili – the middle class if you may, which was made up of merchants, teachers, lawyers, the clergy – who might possibly have the money but none of the titles or rights the Nobles had received or demanded. The last class of people the popolari or municipality – better known as the working class, the farmers, laborers, the mariners. This class had only obligations and no rights.

With their wealth and power, the Venetians built many mansions, actually 'country mansions'. They not only had their country homes, but also their sprawling vineyards and orchards. Even though we were not Venetian, my papaus' family was counted among the past Nobles – the rich, the ruling class – the aristocracy. The males of the family were in banking, therefore in a role of power.

The Venetian rule lasted almost three centuries – it has been told that many Venetians, rich families of the Noble Byzantine origins who had wandered for many years sought refuge on our island – as they were in so many ways like the Israelites having no home land and running away from the spoils and evils of the Turkish occupation. As I have stated previously, the names of the Nobles were placed into a book called the Golden Book (Libro d'oro). But, when the French came in the *late 1790's, they too brought change, a drastic change. For one thing, they ended the three levels of living. There was an uprising against the Nobles and a great cry for change. So, the Golden Book was brought to the city square and along with all the emblems of aristocracy. They were placed in a large heap as a bonfire and burned. All titles were abolished and a new government was established which included the whole island and not just the rich chosen few.*

But, soon the French fled – the Russians came but stayed such a short time, as the Turks grew stronger and began the Turkish/Ottoman Rule. Fortunately for us, our island like others in the Ionian chain, was not ruled by the Turks. We say this with great pride as if you do not know; the mainland was almost destroyed by the Turks; they raped our land and took our babies and children away from the families – many times killing those left behind or allowing them to live with nothing, sometimes starving; then these babies and children were put into camps and taught the Moslem way. As they grew older they were Turks not Greeks – they spoke only the Turkish language and lived the Turkish way of life. They were never told of their birthright – ever. Then, as they developed into young men and women they were given arms to fight; to fight as Turks against their own home land – never knowing that they were killing their ancestors, their families and possibly their own mothers and fathers! What a terrible time for Greece and for the world. As I stated, my home, my Zante was spared. Why? We do not know. Maybe the Turks were so barbaric that it took a lot of time to destroy everything in their sight. Our island was never touched.

In 1864, liberation happened. The Greek flag was raised high above the town, at the castle of Zakynthos which looked out over the bay and the sea. Jubilation filled the air. Free from all foreign rule. Free to be a nation that has been tormented because of its locale. Free to be free.

At one time Zante was grand. It was flowing with beauty; some say with milk and honey. Today, it is something different. I know that the island's beauty is still strong. But, I weep at what it was and what it has become. I am not sorry to tell you about our history. You must know the background of my people so I can tell you my story. Ah, where do I begin? Where do I start? I have papers scattered all about me with stories, bits of news and of course letters of love and sacrifice. I will tell you it all, in good time.

You do understand, I hope that you know that there are two islands next to each other – lying in the Ionian Sea? I want to make sure that you know the difference between them, Kephalonia and Zakynthos. Indeed they are different. But they are also like twins, or as brother/sister...as they are! Zante is dry in the north and very green in the south. It is like a bowl. Kephalonia is bigger than Zante. In fact, it is the largest of all the islands in the Ionian. It stretches long and quite chubby whereas Zante is like a triangle facing downward. The twins though have also had a long history of not liking each other. They seem to be in competition. Why? I do not know. That is not part of my story, just that you must know something about Kephalonia or when I speak of her later, you will not say, "Where is this place?" "Why has it not been talked about before?"

If you go to the northern tip of Zakynthos, you will see Kephalonia, just across the channel. At the port of St. Nikolias you can catch a ferry or even from the port in Zakynthos Town.

Lowering the pages, I felt my head spinning. I rummaged through the box and pulled out The Greek and Turkey Guide Book. Stuck in the pages was a book mark, 'You're good.' Opening up the pages, it lay in front of me... ZAKYNTHOS.

⌘

Standing up I looked around for signs, pictures, stories. Were there any? Yes! I went over to her bedside and lifted a photo. There standing in front of an old church was a man, a woman and in her arms a baby. These people must be my grandmother's father and mother and her, on the island. I turned and went over to the bookshelf next to the chair. I skimmed the books and there it was, a Greek Orthodox Bible. I looked at the crocheted doily on the table, the material was very old and very intricate. It was all here, all the time. How come I never noticed or we never talked about it?

But we had. It never settled into your bones until now.

Nana, I should have listened more carefully.

Once I got downstairs, I found the couch empty and Mom had made it to the kitchen table with a cup of coffee in her hands. 'Mind if I have a cup?'
She nodded and pointed to the coffee pot.

'I, um, was up looking through the box Nana left me, some interesting stuff. She was an interesting person.' Leaning over for the sugar jar, 'a lot of stuff about Greece.' No reaction. Should have expected as much? 'I'm kind of blown away that Nana says she's Greek.' More silence. 'Mom, Nana was Greek or it just my imagination?'

She moved her head a bit as she continued to sip her coffee, 'A little of both actually.'

'Can you tell me or am I, at 39 too *young* to understand.' I then laid the travel book on the table.

A half smile came across her face. 'Was that in the box?'

'Yes.'

She lifted it, 'You'll need to get a newer one, it seems quite old.'

'For what?'

'Oh, you know for information, stuff like that.'

'And the other stuff in the box?'

'Ah, right. Nana's book. She always said she would put it down on paper one day. And she did?'

'Well, I've only got another page and a half, but no I don't think she got it all down. It would be a very small book. She's written mostly about the island, you know the history, where it's located and not much else.'

'She would be upstairs for what seemed like hours typing away on that old typewriter. *Singing with the keys* is what she'd call it. It gave her something to do.'

I gave her that typewriter right after we got the new electric ones at the college. And now those are gone too, the computer has taken over. She never would consider typing on anything except that old Olivetti.' Setting down her coffee cup, it seemed like she was choosing her next words. 'She was Greek, born there and then came over, I guess it would be 1953 or 54.'

'Wait. That's only 50 odd years ago. That means if she was there in 1953, then you were born there also?'

She lifted the cup to her lips.

'Doing the math...you were about...'

'Two when we left.'

⌘

'So, if you're Greek...'

'Then you are also. Yes. But honey, I don't remember much. Once we left and came over here we made America our permanent home. Being that young and being taken away from our home was pretty traumatic. I only vaguely remember anything.'

'Didn't you ever go back? Want to go back?'

'To what? I didn't have any friends. Mom and Dad never expressed any real interest that they wanted to return. I had school, then teaching, and of course a family to raise. Did I want to? I guess some part of me did. If they had wanted to, I probably would have gone.'

'Hmm. Nana may not like computers, but ...' Settling into the large office chair I turned my attention to the screen in front of me and started my search. What came up was an island with beautiful blue water.

'Mom, come here.'

'What dear?'

'You mean to tell me that you left this and never wanted to return?'

Pulling up a chair she sat right down. 'It is beautiful, isn't it? I haven't seen the island in years. And for a two year old, that isn't what I remember.'

'I'm going.'

'What?'

'Of course, if the flights are reasonable.'

'What?'

'I have time left and I think this is what Nana would want me to do.'

I felt a touch on my shoulder as she was getting up to leave. 'A new guide book isn't out of the question, is it now?'

I reached up and touched her hand. 'You can come too.'

'Not now. But, I'm not saying no.'

The internet started sucking me in. The best fare I could find was booking a flight through Denver to Munich and onto Athens.

Well done, dear. The money will be available soon.

I'll just put it on my Visa Nana.

Oh, I hate those cards.

So do I.

Walking back into Nana's room, I went over to the bed and laid down where not 24 hours earlier, her body had been, the tears began to flow. 'I was a very foolish girl, wasn't I?'

Why?

Because you talked and I'm afraid I didn't listen.

Actually, you did listen. You'll find that you'll remember more than you give yourself credit for.

Do you really think that? Look, in one day I've had to say goodbye to you, found thing about you and your past I still don't quite understand and have just booked a trip to a place that is quite foreign to me, it's almost too much. And now, here I am...

And without knowing it, my eyes closed and my body fell asleep.

⌘

The next morning, I heard the phone ring so jumping up to answer it I ran right into mom, 'Mom?'

'I feel so alone.'

I reached over and held her. 'I know.'

The phone kept ringing, but we didn't want to leave.

'Don't you think it's a bit weird that we slept in Nana's bed?'

'No, it actually helped. I saw you in here asleep so I brought in a blanket, a couple pillows and curled up next to you. I needed to be near the only thing I have left.'

'It was just...' I couldn't say it.

'I know.' And she began to cry.

⌘

Even though Nana was loved by many, we chose to hold a small service. Sitting next to me was Mom, and filling the rest of the seats were some of my school friends, some of Nana's friends and Nana's youngest brother Nic.

I had found an old religious card stuck in her Bible, so I read it out loud. 'I will walk alone, and talk alone, but I know you are always beside me.' I thought this strange. How can you be alone, but know that someone is with you? But, I knew this was Nana's way of looking at the world. When I was young she gave me a Bible with an inscription inside, *The sins of the world will keep you from this book, but this book will keep you from the sins of the world.*

After the service and greeting people, we drove home. We drove home in silence. I just couldn't say the words I felt that needed to be said. Mom at one point reached over and touched my hand which rested on the gearshift, squeezing it just a bit. I guess nothing had to be said.

I hadn't gone back to Nana's room, or looked at the box for several days. There were plans to be made like what should be done with Nana's stuff. And my number one project that while I was going to be gone, what would happen to Mom? Each day seemed to be a flurry of things to get done and each night I would walk past Nana's room, but I just couldn't make a detour into it. I didn't even have enough time to do what I really wanted to do and that was to read Nana's diaries as well as search on the internet for more information. I hadn't realized that my time to leave was just a day away. First, I had to get into the attic that we never went into and retrieve the old pair of suitcases dad used to use to travel. Lugging them down the narrow stairs and into my room I started feeling scared. What am I doing? I've committed traveling to Greece but doing this, I must be nuts. Think rationally. Well, with Nana pushing that will not be hard to do.

Dear, if you can't do it, don't do it. That's what your mother would say. But to me, it's simple do it and enjoy the adventure you only live once.

Okay, let the adventure begin. Taking the passport out of the fireproof drawer in the family room I turned and there was Mom looking through some family albums. As I approached I could see that she was touching each face and not hearing me seemingly lost in her own world. I gently slid next to her and laid my head on her shoulder. 'It's going to be quiet here without you.'

'Think I'm crazy?'

'Not in the least.'

'But, what will you do when I'm flying half way around the world?'

'Sift through the years of accumulation and ready myself for the next adventure.'

'Ah, the adventure, I keep hearing that word.'

'It's better than the alternative.'

'Isn't that photo the same one on the wall next to Nana's room?'

'Good eye. Nana as a young woman. As my dad always said, she was quite a looker.'

'And, she was.'

'That she was.' Closing the album she looked up, 'I knew this day would come. I just wasn't as prepared as I thought I'd be. That said, I think this chapter has closed on me, you and this house. We need to open another one. I think that is precisely what you are doing. And, I am proud of you. I mean, I only have a few years left before I retire and here we are going out to venture into the unknown.'

'I can get your passport too.'

'No, not yet. Let me have my alone time with this house and the past. I don't want to do it on my own, but, I have to, understand?'

Leaning my head on her shoulder I whispered, 'understood.'

⌘

Mom stood in the doorway, 'Packed?'

'I think so. I'm really trying to follow the airlines rules. I really wished I knew what to take, but one thing I'm not going to forget is the laptop, my passport and Nana's three diaries.'

'Well, if you're ready, I'll take you to the airport.'

'That won't be necessary. I've already called a taxi. Besides, you know how miserable it is to maneuver around San Francisco International.'

'I don't know why you didn't fly out of Oakland. It is so much easier.'

'Would have been easier, right? I found this in the box with all the other things, have you ever seen it before?' With that, I handed her a silver chain.

'I might have, she did have a lot of jewelry. That's another thing that I will need to sort out while you are gone.'

'Don't get rid of anything until I get home?'

'I'll do my best. What I do promise is that things of value or of the past, I'll put aside.'

'I hate leaving you here to all of this by yourself.'

'I kind of need it.'

Just then the horn from the taxi blared.

I looked over at her. 'You will be okay?'

The horn blared again.

'He's not going to be patient, you'd better hurry.'

I ran to the door and waved at him. Stepping out of the taxi was a very short, older looking man.

'Which airport?'

'SFO. The plane leaves in 2 ½ hours.'

'Then we'd better get going, it might take that long just to get there. How many bags?'

'Just these two.'

Stepping up to the porch he looked them up and down. 'There's a charge to take them to the car.'

'I'll pay.'

He grunted as he headed toward the car and placed the two bags in the truck.

'You'll phone?'

'I'll even do better. I'll get on the computer.'

'All you have to do is go to the big E and click. Never mind. I'll walk you through it when I get to Denver.'

'I love you dear.'

'Me too.'

'If you don't want to leave, I'll take the bags out of the car.'

With a quick hug and a huge kiss, I ran down the steps and into the back seat.

Looking back at the house, I noticed how big it was and how small Mom looked beside it.

Saying goodbye with a wave, she stood as the taxi drove away.

I promise that whatever I need to find, I'll bring it home for the two of us.

⌘

I hate it when the taxi driver talks when you don't want to be talked to. And that's exactly what happened.

Here I am trying to sort out everything in my head, such as if the passport is up to date, do I have the right credit cards, then driver's license is with me, what good will that do, guess I'll find out, my cell phone, the list goes on. I kept nodding my head trying to ensure that he knows I'm in the conversation as well as keeping my head on task. Suddenly, out of nowhere I said, 'I don't even know if my cell phone works overseas.'

'What?'

'I'm sorry. I didn't mean to interrupt. But I truly don't know if my cell phone works overseas.'

'What country did you say you were headed to?'

'Greece via Germany.'

'Well, do you have T Mobile?'

'I...um...'

'Turn it off then you switch it back on.'

I did what he suggested. 'Yes!'

'T Mobile is from Germany. When you have time at the airport have T Mobile switch it the international mode. Oh, did you bring an adapter?'

'No, I don't have an adapter. Oh, wait, do you mean to plug this in the wall?'

'Yeah, that's okay you can pick them at the airport too.'

'You really aren't prepared for this, are ya?'

Then it hit me. No, I wasn't.

'You said you were flying?'

'International.'

'Right.' He pulled the cab up to the curb and after bringing my bags out and handing them over to the sky cap he turned to me, 'that will be $47.50.'

'Okay...hold on.' Pulling out my purse I found a $50. 'Will that do?'

'If that's all the tip you can give, yeah, that'll do.'

In a flash he was gone. Wasn't a $50 enough? Do taxi drivers declare their tips? I am so not organized for this!

The sky cap interrupted me with, 'Thank you for flying the friendly skies, I noticed that your bags weren't tagged. Here's two name tags for you to fill out, could I have your reservation sheet please?'

'I don't need to go inside?'

'Nope, we can handle it all out here. Everything, except security clearance. You know, 9/11 stuff.'

'Right. I remember.'

With bags and myself checked in, I headed for my gate with that wonderful pit stop called security. 'Don't forget to take off your shoes too.' I lifted the lap top over my shoulder and placed my purse next to me.

Can't be too careful. I shook my head, 'What in the hell have I gotten myself into?'

⌘

With moments to spare, I mean moments, as I had forgotten you are supposed to be at the airport two hours ahead for international...it must have been my legs or something because the sky captain was ensuring I got on the flight, I ducked into the travel store, got me an international plug for both my lap top and my phone. After getting T Mobile straightened out the 'all boarding' announcement was being mumbled over the intercom.

I clipped down to the gate, down the gang plank and into the plane. 'Row 12 seat A?'

'Yes, this side.' Some polite but overly made up stewardess nodded at me.

Finding my seat I put the lap top case in the overhead and sat down. I drew a deep breath.

The plane was filling up and looking over I noticed an older man sitting next to me. He smiled, and I smiled back. He seems friendly – wouldn't it be weird if he was on the same plane all the way to Athens!

After the emergency announcements , in flight videos and take off, I felt my shoulders drop as well as my head right into the window well and off to sleep I went.

'Miss. Miss?'

Coming out of my sleep, I looked up. 'Yes?'

'We're landing in Denver, let's make sure your seat belt is fastened?'

'Ah, sure.'

The nice gentleman next to me smiled again, but this time said, 'You've been a sleep all the way from San Francisco.'

'Oh, I hope I didn't snore.'

'No madam, I think you are too polite for that.' Disembarking that plane to go to another terminal to get on another plane I started to feel my flying wings were back. It had been several years since I made an international trip, but once you've done it, you remember the hang of it.

⌘

Boarding again was a breeze and once again I was sitting near the front of the plane, and once again, the gentleman I flew with from San Francisco was sitting next to me. Was this a coincidence?

'Again we sit together.'

'And, this time I will be a better traveling companion.'

'So, you have slept enough? It is a long flight to Munich.'

I truly had forgotten to look at my tickets, 'how long is it?'

'Almost 9 ½ hours.'

'There'll be another nap, or two.' I chuckled at my remark, why? 'Excuse me, but you have an accent that I'm not familiar with.'

'Ah, we all have accents. I'm Turkish.'

I would have never guessed. 'Turkish. What part?'

'I have a home in Istanbul, and another home in Izmir.'

'Two homes?'

'One work, one my family home.'

Through a dinner, a snack, two horrible B movies, CNN and then breakfast I learned about his life. He also educated me on the Ottoman Empire (the whole thing Nana wrote was making more sense now), some Greek history, the EU and of course the almighty euro. I would have said dollar, but it's not so mighty currently.

I kept telling him that as Americans we aren't educated in world history such as that of the Ottoman Empire – especially the way he explained it.

The tables then were turned on me. What do I tell him or anyone else? Would anyone ever believe when I tell them that I'm on a wild goose chase sent by my dead grandmother? I moved my blanket around and said, 'I'm headed to Greece to, as you might say, to dig up some old bones.'

'Ah, that sounds interesting. Do you know where you are 'digging up the bones'?'

'Yes, an island called Zakynthos.'

'I have not heard of such a place. Is it close to Santorini?'

'I don't know.' I pulled out my Greek/Turkish book and he smiled. I found Santorini in the Aegean side, close to Israel and Turkey but finding Zakynthos was a bit daunting this time. 'Oh, here, it's between Italy and Greece.'

'This I do not know. I have never been. Ah, but Corfu...yes, that is where there is a large casino. Yes. Now, the island is on this side (he now was pointing at Santorini, Crete, Rhodes) is very dry so maybe these islands over here are greener because they are more protected?'

He kept bringing up questions that I had no answers for. I knew where I was going, I hoped and that was about it.

By the time we landed in Munich, he handed me his business card and told me, 'Look me up if you wish. My wife makes a wonderful kebab.'

⌘

I had little less than an hour before my Aegean Airlines flight was to leave. I went over to information and asked them if they knew of any flights or anything to the island of Zakynthos.

The young man from behind the desk smiled, 'I know not of this place.'

Better start reading that guide of mine...not too many people 'know of this place.' Once on the plane the 2 ½ hour flight went by quickly. The airplane was crowded with all sorts of languages. Maybe it's Greek. Then it hit me, oh, my god, What do I say? They have to speak English. I mean it's the world's most spoken language. And then, maybe not. Time to study. Fortunately, the guide had what I was looking for. My inner voice started in, 'If I take the Bus 12 from the airport to Syntagma Square, change to Bus 51 which will take me to the central bus station, then I can catch another bus to the island via a ferry. Whew, this better work. Can't I just fly? The guide stated that flights to the island of Zakynthos are only operated by Olympic Air if from Athens. There is one flight in the morning and one in the evening. I'll take the bus/ferry that way I'll see some sights and bone up on my knowledge.' I began to chuckle and without thinking spoke out loud. 'Knowledge, yeah right.'

Landing in Athens seemed easy. The shuttle bus that took us to the terminal which was crowded and languages were darting past me left and right. I might be wrong about the 'universal' language. Eyes darted at me like I was a piece of meat. And it wasn't just the men, it seemed like everyone took a look. 'Maybe this was foolish, single woman traveling by herself.' Finding my way to the carousel for my luggage, I searched for the customs area. No customs? People just walked out into the open air. So not like the USA. With that, I dragged the suitcases behind me and walked out of departures and right to the bus stop, no change, maybe go to the metro?

Euro's. Thank goodness for exchange booths. The fifty dollar bill was returned with what amounted to 32.00 euro's. Okay. Certainly this is proving that Greece is not a third world country anymore, is it?

Heading through the turnstile and down the escalator, the metro was seconds from departure. Once on the train, I fitted my bags in next to me and I sat down with nothing less than grace.

Looking around I couldn't help but notice that the train was cleaner than the BART back home. And the voice overhead spoke in both English and what I assumed was Greek. The sign over head declared the stops and as I looked out I felt a twinge in my stomach, what have I done?

Then it happened. Looking out over the landscape I saw Athens and yes, the Parthenon. Standing high on a hill in the center of this vast city was the temple of Athena. I was awestruck. That building has stood there since the fifth century BC; withstood bombings, fires, earthquakes and yes, it's damaged, but it's still magnificent. I was brought out of my haze by what I thought was a voice over head declaring "Syntagma Square."

I looked up and flashing on the reader board was just that, so grabbing everything I could in one fell sweep, I made my way wearily off the metro.

Making my way through the maze, I found myself coming up out into the city and a large square. The hustle and bustle of the city as well as the awkwardness of my baggage nearly did me in.

Wobbling down a road full of pot holes, tugging at my baggage and almost out of breath, I set my bags down and looked around. This is the bus station? Now what? There was a hustle and bustle that could cause any sane person a thought to step back on the bus I had just stepped off of and head back home. Nothing was in English and a bit confusing. Even though my impressions of Athens being of a fairly clean city, that was now changing, to a truly dirty, filthy and smelly urban area. It was like being in Harlem when it was down and out, or a bad side of Detroit; and this is the 'main' terminal? As I stood taking it 'all in', I was being pushed back and forth by people not unlike me, but they all seemed to know where to go. Scanning the signs attached to the ceiling it finally dawned on me how to read Greek or at least interpret it. The word Zakynthos with the number 38 was to my left and looking down I saw a stall. No joke, a stall. And there at the stall was a small house that I entered, 'Zakynthos?'

'Ne.'

'English?'

'Yes.'

'Great. I would like to get to Zakynthos.'

'7 euro ferry and 24 euro bus fare.'

'31 euro?'

'31 euro.'

Handing over the fare I was handed two papers.

The pink/white one was, 'Ferry, no seat.' The yellow/blue was 'bus, seat 10.'

'How long?'

'Bus to Zakynthos is 16:45.'

16:45...come on Denny military time, 'ah, 4:45.' Looking down at my watch, 5 hours. 'Thank you.' Turning to leave, 'oh, where do I wait?'

'Outside.'

Stepping out of the building I noticed a row of chairs on both sides of the door. 'Wait five hours.' Setting my bags next to me, the waiting game began.

⌘

Hours passed. Buses came and went. It was odd seeing all these new buses in a rundown terminal. Why was that so? How could you have a wonderful looking bus in a horribly grimy bus terminal? No one seemed to mind, except for me. Most looked like locals, traveling to and fro. Why didn't anyone seem to mind? The airport was beautiful, the metro was beautiful, but this? Then it dawned on me. The Olympics. Ah. Money had been poured into appearances and maybe it just ran out, or they didn't expect most travelers to ever travel down here. In any case, my obsession with this cleared away from my thoughts as I started nodding off. The hours were taking a toll on me. At three, a bus rolled up into the stall and the sound of air brakes woke me out of my slumber. People climbed off the bus and then it closed its doors. Within the next hour, the once bare area around me filled up with various people carrying bags, boxes and cages. At almost precisely 4:30 the doors flung open and everyone scurried to get their items into the baggage holder and onto the bus. I handed my bags over to a gentleman who seemed to be organizing this mayhem, then I made my way with the herd of others onto the bus. Under my breath I kept saying seat 10. How in the world do I find my seat number? I started counting. It has to be at least the third row…just then an older woman behind me started pushing at my arm and pointing upwards. Ah, under the small luggage carrier were numbers. I smiled and moved forward. I don't think she cared about me as much as to get me out of the way. Once in my seat, I collapsed. My body seemed to say, 'Well, how do you like your journey so far?' What my ears heard was a voice asking, 'Excuse me, could you move your personal effects?' Looking up there stood a truly respectable looking man. Dressed quite nicely and trying to be, well, nice. 'Did you pay for both of these seats or just one?'

⌘

'I am so sorry. It's just been a long trip.'

'Ah.' As he sat down. 'You still have a four hour bus trip and another hour on the ferry before our destination. You are going to Zakynthos, correct?'

'Yes.'

'Then we are in luck.'

'Luck? I wouldn't consider you lucky sitting next to me.'

'And why is that?'

'Considering that I left San Francisco yesterday and I haven't had a decent sleep or shower.'

'Ah.'

'Just don't breathe too deep.'

We both laughed. It felt good to laugh. It was true that I hadn't taken a shower in a full day, which was very rare for me, but I had brushed my teeth, checked my makeup and hair on the plane before we landed. Running around with airplane hair is not my style.

'San Francisco to Zakynthos?'

'Yes. Long story.'

'Have you ever been?'

'Zakynthos? No, have you?'

'Many times, I go because of business.'

'Oh?'

'And family.'

The front door of the bus closed tight, and with the engine started, it backed up and started weaving out of the building and out into the busy streets of Athens.

'Yes, I am working with local vineyards to bottle wine of Zante and sell it abroad.'

I began to wonder if I should be so friendly with him. Here I was a single woman in a foreign land talking to a stranger, I looked down and did not see a ring on his left hand only on his right. Looking back up he caught my eye.

'You are wondering if we should speak?'

He being forthright was not what I was expecting, 'Yes. Wine?' My brain and mouth didn't seem to function together. He wasn't too attractive, a five o'clock shadow made his face look darker than I suspected he actually was and his suit was better than, Macy's. I could just hear my mother's voice, 'Still dear, you cannot be too careful.' But with him sitting next to me for four hours, how not careful could I be?

He chuckled. 'You are tired. I'm sorry for making you talk.' He lifted his hands up. 'I must tell you that no, I am not married, true. But like most Greek males we like our women. We flirt but most of the time it is very harmless. Rest now, we shall talk later.' With that, he pulled out his brief case and began to shuffle papers.

I turned toward the window and pressed my head against the pane. In no time my head was cleared of any thoughts of Athens, Greece, Nana or this man sitting next to me.

⌘

'Signómi.'

I felt a hand on my shoulder, turning I saw this face, I thought I recognized.

'Miss?'

Pulling my body and thoughts together I looked around. Ah, the bus. 'Yes?'

'We have stopped for 15 minutes. You should get up, have a Nescafe."

'Nescafe', the powdered stuff?'

He laughed. 'I guess.'

'I'm a true boil-it-in-the-pot kind of girl.'

'I do not know what you mean. What I am trying to tell you is that this is a time to take a walk. We still have another two hours to go.'

'Oh, get up and stretch my legs.' I wasn't doing much better was I? Reaching the door, I looked out and saw people looking over a ledge. Instead of heading for the café, I went to see what they were looking at. There over the ledge was a vast canal.

'I heard you gasp. The first time looking down at the canal at Corinth?' came a voice from behind me.

'Like in the Bible, Corinthians?'

'Yes and no. Yes. This is the land of the Corinthians. And some say, who Paul talks about. And this is the 'Isthmos Canal of Corinth'. Quite far down?'

'Yes, and it looks like there's no real structure to it. Like, most places I've seen which have cement walls to hold the dirt back.'

'Ah, yes, this one doesn't. That is truly 'dirt' that you see. It took approximately 2,495 years from inception to completion in 1893. It was decided after the building of the Suez Canal that it finally could be done. The work was started after many mishaps in 1869. I must tell you that when the Nazi's were leaving our mainland, they tried to shut it down, putting I believe, five railroad cars in the canal as well as setting explosives to its sides. It took almost four years to reopen.'

'The Nazis?'

'World War II, they occupied this part of Greece.'

'Things you do not learn from your world history class.'

'Probably because there were other things the Nazis were doing that were much worse and that affected the whole world.'

'This is absolutely a work of art. The vast narrowness, the orangey brown color and look how long it is.'

'Indeed.'

'I knew Hitler's military went into France, Italy and Russia, but Greece also? I don't think that is taught in our history books unless I had forgotten something.'

We started walking toward the coffee shop, 'Remember, Hitler and that Nazi invasion went all the way into Africa.'

'True.' I started chuckling, 'he truly was the twentieth century little Napoleon wasn't he?'

'He may have been even worse.'

As we approached the counter, he asked me to go first, but I excused myself and headed to the ladies room. When I returned no one was waiting at the counter, so I ordered my first cup of Nescafe' in many years but remembering how it tasted ordered it with a lot of sugar.

I looked around but didn't find him in the café so I headed back out toward the bus and the canal.

'I see you have found Nescafe".'

'When in Rome...'

He chuckled and before I could correct myself he said, 'I know that expression.'

The first taste of the contents from the cup nearly made me spit it out, but "when in Rome" so I sipped and began to talk. 'I still don't remember Greece being mentioned in Hitler's conquest. I seem to remember that either his travesties were maybe larger in other countries and that Greece was figured so prominently. You know, almost skipped.'

'Not skipped as much as not talked about. Ah, we are ready to leave.'

Approaching the bus he stood to drink the rest of his coffee. It was just too hot to drink quickly so I proceeded to the bus. He noticed what I was about to do and yelled. 'Miss!' Again he yelled, 'Miss San Francisco!'

I looked up and around and then saw him coming toward me. 'Did you just call me Miss San Francisco?'

'Yes, because I do not know your name.'

'I don't know yours either.'

The bus blew its horn and he put his hand out, 'You can't take the cup on the bus.'

'Oh.' In one swoop he took it, threw it in the trash and showed me onto the bus. As we pulled out onto the road I turned to him, 'I didn't know.'

'Only bottled water, its cleaner that way.'

'The first part of our trip, did I miss much?'

'No, but you did sleep. I felt you needed to close your eyes to this world and rest, and you did.'

Leaning down to touch my belongings, he commented, 'No one has touched anything that I promised.'

'It's not that, I just feel a little out of sorts.'

The bus started climbing mountains and the chatter of cell phones kept going off. We talked about wine, his life and a bit of San Francisco, especially the wine country of the Napa Valley.

'You do know that many Zakythonian's now live in San Francisco?'

'Really. Why? Ah, do you not think one history lesson a day is enough?'

'I'm curious why anyone would travel half way around the world...' and then it hit me, 'but I'm doing it right now, aren't I?'

He smiled. 'I see you also answer your own questions.'

'Yes, and I generally stop before anyone else can hear me say them out loud.'

Looking out the road rambled on, getting closer to the water.

'Ah, we are approaching Patras. See the new bridge?'

'Wow, that is absolutely beautiful. However, it doesn't look like it goes to anywhere.'

'Ah, but it does. You are correct though that it only looks like it goes to the other side of the river and ends, a place to nowhere. I promise you, it leads to the upper part of Greece up to the second largest city in Greece, Thessaloniki.'

'Say that word one more time?'

'Thessaloniki. Some say it is where Paul of the New Testament wrote to in his letters entitled Thessalonicans.'

'Corinth for Corinthians and now Thessaloniki for Thessalonians, should have studied more of my history and Bible.'

'Many Greeks take these things for granted. It's history of the old. So what if it is here in our land, maybe like you and the Statue of Liberty?'

'Miss Liberty herself, all the way from France.'

'I see you know your history.'

'The French will not let us forget. And why should they? She is absolutely beautiful, a welcoming beacon for so many who did not have such a great life in their own countries.'

'I have only seen her in pictures.'

'I have seen her in person; she is absolutely amazing standing in the harbor with her hand held high. What I like the most is that Frederic Bartholdi made her also humble by having her hold a book. Do you know what is inscribed on the book?'

'Justice for all? Or welcome all?'

'Actually, just July 4, 1776.'

'Simple.'

'Very.'

Just then the bus slowed and turned onto a small road. 'Ah, we are almost to Kellini.'

'The port?'

'Very good, then onto the ferry.'

The bus swerved back and forth through slender streets that seemed that only a small car could travel. I was expecting the sides to scrape as we passed, but somehow we entered the small port where there stood two large ferries. The commotion on the bus was amazing. People were standing, pushing, grabbing even before the bus stopped.

'Why the commotion?'

'Yes, why?' was the only reply I received.

The bus stopped and after most left the bus, I started to get up then yelled at my companion, 'what about our bags?'

'Just bring your purse, everything else stays on the bus.'

'But, isn't the bus leaving?'

'No. It will pick us up at the docks of Zakynthos town and then into the bus station.'

Strange I thought, but oh well, off the bus I trotted with all the others and then onto the ferry.

⌘

Ropes were being pulled on board and a loud screech echoed as the metal ramp retracted into the vessel.

As the ferry launched away from the dock, I sat down and looked out back toward the dock. 'Goodbye mainland, what an adventure you have given to me. What more is going to come?'

The rumbling of the engine pulling the ferry out to the open water slowly brought me back to reality. The engines pulling the large vessel past the jetty made of rock then out onto the open water. The ferry shook like a tremor of an earthquake – steady without letting up; almost like being on an old train. The noises of people talking the different languages – families enjoying their time together, business men planning their meetings, young loves expressing themselves, and old people with sun wrinkled faces telling stories without speaking a word. The sound of the engine, the people, the water all humming various sounds as in one harmony with the rocking of the ferry you could almost feel like someone who should belong.

A hand touched my shoulder as the ferry rocked a bit. 'Oh! Whoa…what was that?'

The man from the bus sat next to me, 'Oh, that? The sea is not as smooth once you are out on it. It has a bit of a rocking motion like when you take your hand and push a cradle, or when you push a swing – ever so gently.'

'I thought I had lost you.'

'The sea is vast, but this boat is not.'

Just then a young boy, no older than two walked past with a tall man – was it his father? The young boy carrying a small orange car – his voice sang as he walked toward the woman seated a couple tables away. When he saw her, he ran, speaking quickly.

'He's excited about his new toy.'

'I figured as much, how easy it is to please the young.' What did I know of that? Would I ever know? The boat started taking on a storybook essence to me. I, an observer to lives I could only observe. To the left of me, on the other side of the room a couple was seated. The kiss exchanged was not of lovers but of a people comfortable with each other. The man nuzzled into her neck. She laughed just slightly. Then she reached into her back pack and retrieved what looked like a book, a diary, similar to Nana's. She handed it to him, taking it, he opened to a blank page, began writing with passion not stopping except when she got up to leave him. He looked up slowly, smiled but didn't stop his writing.

The table opposite was another couple, older reviewing maps, guide book, planning where to find their treasures. She reached and touched his hand, gently tapping it either without changing what they were doing. In love? Maybe, but if so, it was definitely an older love.

The young woman returned – she was carrying two hot cups of what appeared to be coffee. He placed the pen in the spine of the book and closed it accepting the cup; she settled back into her seat. Interesting it wasn't the man who got the drink – maybe she went to the washroom then decided to surprise him? Maybe she always does this? She let out a chuckle –

'Signómi? I'm sorry, excuse me?'

'I was just noticing those people over there, the look like tourists. Probably planning or trying to figure out where they were bound.'

'Ke? (And?)'

'I have no idea.'

'Nothing?'

But my eye caught the young man handing the diary to the young woman. He stood up, kissed her on the forehead and left. She opened it up and started reading, flipping the page to read more. Her face was almost flawless, clean of wrinkles, ah to be <u>that</u> young again! Thin framed, her blond hair pulled back, her eyes gazed up to mine, she gave a half smile, then reached for her drink.

I smiled back and tried to act like I had just looked over. Did she know that I had been looking for awhile?

Looking around, I noticed that the couple with the maps had disappeared, or moved. The little boy was still playing with his car, running the wheels on the vacant seat between the two older people.

'A ship out to sea.'

'Not quite a ship.'

The young man passed our table back to his; he walked up talking quickly Were they English? Suddenly, the car sped under my legs – past me and into the corner. The little boy slowly walked past, his head barely seen at the top of the chairs. Shyly he reached down, retrieved his car, then over to the tall woman. Sliding onto the chair, he turned and smiled.

Smiling back I said out loud, 'Things just get away from us.'

I was startled by the sound of the diary being closed loudly, and then put back into the satchel. Looking up sharply, I tried to avert my eyes; I noticed several pictures on the wall. I could still feel the young woman's eyes on me.

'Tell me about these photos.'

'The old photos of the boat. I don't think anyone notices them anymore. There mostly to show the tourist what they are going to see, or help them remember what they have already saw.'

'The locals don't care?'

'Why should they? It's part of them.'

'That photo.'

'The first one to your right? That is Solomos Square and the statue is of our National poet, Dionysios Solomos. That is also where the museum, library and theatre of Zakynthos are.'

'Impressive.'

'You will see them and think that they are small. You will know about the history, and understand then why the islanders are very proud of them.'

'Tell me, you said National poet?'

'He was born on the island and is known for writing the Greek national anthem, "Anthem to Liberty"'.

'Do you know any of it, in English of course?'

Without missing a beat he began first in Greek and then in English 'Σε γνωρίζω από την κόψη του σπαθιού την τρομερή, σε γνωρίζω από την όψη που με βία μετράει τη γη. Απ' τα κόκκαλα βγαλμένη των Ελλήνων τα ιερά, και σαν πρώτα ανδρειωμένη, χαίρε, ω χαίρε, Ελευθεριά!; I shall always recognize you by the dreadful sword you hold, as the Earth, with searching vision, you survey with spirit bold. From the Greeks of old whose dying brought to birth our spirit free, now, with ancient valor rising, let us hail you, oh liberty!'

'That is beautiful.'

'Indeed.'

I closed my eyes and just sat there, saying the words out loud 'Let us hail you, oh liberty!' When I opened my eyes I had almost forgotten I was with anyone, let alone in the midst of a state room on a ferry.

'Maybe I should give you a Greek lesson?'

I looked at my watch.

'There is plenty of time.'

'I would like that. I feel like a duck out of water, but I must also tell you that I am a bit tired so if I don't catch on right away there's a reason.'

'I understand. I'll try to start off easy.'

'Please do.'

'So let's start with one you will use a lot.'

'And that is?'

'Hello.'

⌘

For the next 45 minutes we were engaged with words like Ne (yes), Ohi (no), okay (okay), Yasus (hello and or goodbye), Kalimeria (good morning), Signómi (excuse me or sorry) and of course Efharisto (thank you).

'How do you know so much?' 'How come you are being so nice to me?' My questions just kept coming.

'Actually, I, like some; were born in another country. Me? Australia. You see, in the late 60's, Australia was booming and didn't have many skilled laborers so it called upon Europe. My father thought that this was his golden opportunity so he took his young bride, my mother and lived there for almost twenty years. During that time, they had me and my brother. However, when in 1994, when I turned 16, we moved back. My father said, "We are going home. You will be raised properly. You are Zakynthoian."

'Now we have a problem. You see, all the years my father worked in Australia he paid into a pension fund. However, now that we have moved back to Greece, he has fought to get his pension. Why? Well, there is no pension agreement between the governments of Greece and Australia. And, my father is ill, 61 and bedridden. I have talked with the Australian government, they say, "if he moved back here for two years or even moved to Cypress and lived, he would obtain his full retirement."
I try to tell them of his illness, that he can't be moved and they just say, "Then talk to your government." After several years of phone calls, letters and screaming my mother asks, "Can't they just talk to each other? Here a man is dying and needs to get proper care." Nothing.'

'What will happen?'

'Ella. (come on) Presently, we lose. He lives on the little pension he has made since moving back and I will help where I can. Yes, I come for work but also for family.'

'You don't live here on the island full time though, do you?'

'Ohi, I live in Athens and come back and forth.'

A long pause endured between us. I could tell that this conversation wasn't easy. Then he spoke again, with a renewed voice. 'This time, I am also going to a conference in Zakynthos Town, and I will see my father, mother and spend some time with them.'

'They probably will be very happy to see their son. Now, what about the other pictures, this one that has palm trees?'

His eyes caught mine. I couldn't tell what he was thinking, probably 'American women are strange!'

Before I could speak he looked away toward the picture 'This is not typical. Like you would say Hawaii or the Canary Islands, I am guessing that the picture is from a resort.'

'And that one there is the harbor?'

'Zakynthos Town, the Strata Marina...'

'It's beautiful.'

'Almost all Greek Islands have a port – this one is Zante Town...'

'Zante Town?'

'It's what the locals call it – it is a what you say...'

'A nick name? We call San Francisco – Frisco or San Fran...'

'Bravo!'

I was truly beginning to enjoy his company.

'You are learning.'

'I feel that I must.'

'Come, let us walk out onto the deck and see if we can see the disappearance of Kellini and the arrival of the island.'

⌘

His hand lay gently on my back. Somehow it didn't feel strange.

There was a slight breeze which hit me as I arrived onto the side of the ship. The sun was moving ever so slightly higher into the sky, 'Ah, this is more like it! There was a bit too much smoke for me in there.'

'Yes, we seem to like our cigarettes,' he said as he was reaching into his pocket. 'You don't mind, do you?' A Marlboro pack was slowly taken out of his breast jacket pocket.

'Out here, no.' I stepped closer to the railing and breathed in. The water hit against the side of the ferry as we headed toward our destination.

'Why didn't you fly?' came from his mouth after he let out his first puff of the cigarette. 'Wouldn't it have been easier?'

I couldn't help but smile. That was going to be my question to him, 'I think it's because I wanted to get a feel of the country, see what this place was like, and you?'

'Ah yes, me. A businessman who takes a ferry, you think it's because I am not without means?' He took the cigarette and placed it slowly into his mouth, as if every moment with the cigarette must be savored.

'I don't mean to pry.' Right then I felt like I maybe shouldn't have asked. How foolish of me, asking questions of someone who I really didn't know other than for sharing an early morning bus ride to an island I had never visited.

'I enjoy this.'

'That's all?'

'Come look.' He stepped closer to me, 'Over there that is the mainland.' His finger pointed left, 'and there, you cannot see it but in that direction is Mt. Olympus, the highest mountain in Greece.'

I couldn't help but chuckle.

'What?'

'There's a Mt. Olympus in San Francisco, too.'

'Really?'

'Yes, it's about 560 feet...'

'About 170 meters, Hmm, Greece's Mt. Olympus is approximately 9,500 feet or 2,900 meters.'

'No comparison.'

'None, it is however, quite interesting that this is another similarity between our two places.'

'Amazing.'

He started to walk toward the bow of the boat and pointed right, 'see that ferry in the distance, it's headed to Kephalonia. And that?' He was about to finish when people started standing up as if for an evacuation. 'What's happening?'

The engines started growing louder, the rumbling sharper.

'We are here.'

The island was coming into sight. He threw up his hands and walked toward a group of men.

My head was spinning...'we're here?' The island grew closer and my anxiety grew larger. 'Okay Nana, this is for the both of us. Please be my guide.'

⌘

I felt pushed and shoved in many directions, but it didn't feel wrong. My body continued with the flow and on exiting the ferry I could not help but gasp. 'It's beautiful Nana...' Almost forgetting my footing, I tried to locate someone, anyone from the bus; finally a red and blue scarf was headed toward a bus. 'That's the one woman from the front seat.' I barely made it onto the bus, when the doors closed and we were whisked past the harbor, through winding streets and various alleys, almost hitting signs, cars and people. The man I had ridden with was not on the bus. I began to panic. 'Calm down, Denny. True, you are all alone in a foreign country where you have just barely begun to learn a word or two of its language...but, you've made it this far, right?'

The bus slowed to a stop and again people hurried to get off the bus. 'Why is everyone in such a hurry? Did they really have to be someplace quickly? I feel like I'm on BART on a weekday morning or a Friday afternoon!' I waited to be the last person off the bus, then proceeded around to gather my luggage. I stood up and leaned backward a bit, 'This traveling is for the birds! I'm pooped.'

Looking up and down the street, 'Which way? Let's see the streets are going north and south...north.' And off I went, all the while thankful that I hadn't brought any more luggage. Passing storefront after storefront, and door fronts and I nearly fell over myself. After a brief stop I looked up. 'There's a Northern Exposure... here? It's surely a rip off store.' As I trudged on a large sign hit my eye, the Strata Marina. It makes sense...a Strata Marina on the Strata Marina! Tugging my bags I climbed the steps, pushed at the door and then another door before I arrived in a wonderful lobby.

'Kalimeria!' came from somewhere...and what do I say in response? There standing behind a large counter was a nicely dressed man. 'Ya?'

The only thing that I could bring forth out of my mouth was, 'English?'

At that precise moment a hand touched my arm. 'More lessons I see, let me.'

The man from the bus, How did...?

He walked past me, up to the desk and began talking. Still fighting with my bags, I tried to follow the conversation; the only word I even had a remote idea of being said was 'ohi'. Which means...and without thinking I shouted, 'NO!'

It seemed like the whole room, no, the whole world, stopped and looked at me.

He turned, 'You do not want a room by yourself?'

I could feel my face...my whole body turn beet red. 'I'm sorry. I was, fighting with my bags and didn't want them to fall.'

With a suspicious look, he then smiled and once again was deep in conversation with the desk clerk. I have to learn some of this language or else I'm going to sink faster than I can swim. I stepped up next to this savior out of nowhere and touched his arm, thinking this is how it is done. He did it for me, right? 'Single room.'

He smiled to the clerk, then to me. 'There is a convention here this day. All the rooms are booked except mine and I am trying to get you, a single room. I also want it to face the marina so your experience here will be one you will always remember. Now, do you have your passport and of course, a credit card? I will pursued him to make this happen.'

Handing over my passport and a credit card, I waited. Within minutes and much Greek, which sounded more like shouting than a civil conversation, I was handed back my credit card.

'What about my passport?'

'Ohi. You will not get it back until you have paid your bill in full upon departure consider it the hotel's insurance that you will honor your stay. I have said you are staying one week?'

'A week will be a good jumping off point.'

'You will be jumping off then? I'm sorry I do not understand.'

'It's a figure of speech. What I meant to say is that one week will be a good starting point for me to get to know the island, where and what I am truly doing here. So I have a room?'

'Ne.'

'Yes?'

'Bravo!'

'Isn't bravo actually Italian?'

'It works the same in Greek too.'

'Bravo!' I shouted, as he handed me my key.

With everything in tow, I followed him to the elevator.

Ding went the bell, then the door opened, 'Let me allow you to go first.'

'Thank you.'

With both of us inside and the door closing, I turned, 'I can't remember how to say thank you.'

'Efharisto.'

'I'll get it....'

'You'll have to.'

He pushed three and off we went. Slowly. The elevator was no more than 5' by 7' and with two people and three suitcases, things were close.

'I'm Denise, Denny for short. I've been meaning to tell you from the moment we were on the bus together, but well...'

'And my name is Yiannis, or as you would say John.'

I reached out to greet him when the elevator's bell rang.

'Ah, here we are.' The door opened and John pulled his bag, holding the door open for me. Walking down the corridor, he began to chuckle.

'Is there something wrong?'

'No, it's just that we find ourselves next to each other.'

'Really.'

'Yes, your room is right next to mine. And no, there is no door between.'

I had to take a second look at him. What did that really mean?

'Efharisto?'

'Parakaló.'

'What does that mean?'

'You're welcome.'

'So, I got it right?'

'Ne.'

'Baby steps.'

He started laughing as he turned to leave. 'Baby steps?'

'Another figure of speech.'

'You American's...have so much to learn and it looks like I have to learn a couple of sayings too. Ahdio.'

'What?'

'Goodbye.'

'Oh, right. I think I will have a nice bath and rest. It has been a long day or two...I can't remember.'

As the door was about to close, he said, 'Breakfast is served downstairs in the morning. That is included in your room. There are plenty of restaurants, taverna's around for you to eat from. Now, I must leave, I have a conference to go to.'

The door closed, the room was dark. Where is the light switch? It clicked on and off and nothing. I ran to the door and fumbling I found the handle, opening it I yelled, 'Yiannis?'

His door opened a bit, 'Ne?'

'How do you turn on the lights?'

'Did you see a slot by the front door? Just slide your key into it and they will come on.'

'Again, efharisto.'

'Ne. Ne. Ne.' His door closed as did mine.

The lights came on just as he said.

⌘

⌘ Nana ⌘

7 April
Today is my birthday. I am eight today. I have received the greatest gifts from Mama and Papa, a diary. With this gift I have become a writer.

10 April
Papa says there is rumor of war. I fear that he might be right.
Mama says that I shouldn't worry. We are safe.

15 April
Today is Holy Saturday.
Today we break jugs.
Mama says there is much evil to be taken care of.

29 April
Yasus diary. You are my friend. Daddy took me down to the ferry. Mama says I can only go with him. Today was a treat.

1 May
I will write in my diary every day, you are my friend.

  I was born Anastasia, or Anna for short, to two wonderful people, Soula and Nionios on the 5th day of April 1928. My young life was spent in a two story building where my father's shop was on the main floor and we resided in the apartment above in the middle part of Zakynthos Town. The building which was handed down to my father from his father was made of cement, cinder blocks and the exterior shown bright with yellow and white stucco. When asked, 'Where do you live?' Our response would be, 'Do you know the building with the hand carved double doors and the large balcony with the wrought iron scrolled veranda? That is our home.' Why you ask, is the description important? Ah, because no other building in our section of town was as simple or as grand as ours. Mama would always say, 'The Venetians gave us a jewel and we must be good stewards of it.' After the morning meal, she would sweep the front step and the balcony and if possible, she would place flowers on the balcony-'a jewel should always looked polished.'

Papa was a good, hard working man. A man who rose with the sun each morning and as he made his way into the family area he would find coffee and toast that Mama had prepared for him. 'If your body is readied for the day, you will succeed,' was her motto. After spending time with all of us, he would find his way down the stairs, unlock the door and invite the sun in.

The shop was open each day at seven thirty sharp except for Fridays and Saturdays. Why Fridays and Saturdays? Papa always had his reasons. And those days Sunday through Thursday, he would close for four hours from one o'clock to five o'clock (sometimes six depending on the heat of the day) and come upstairs, to have lunch and of course a mesimeriano or ypnaco, (a nap).

A nap during the day? Ne! That refreshes you for the remainder of the day. I have never known a day when a nap wasn't taken by each and every member of the family and of the whole town. Why would a shop be open during these hours? Could you not do your banking or shopping before one o'clock or after six?

The shop closed by nine to ensure we had a family meal together and maybe a stroll. Papa would take us out onto the Strata Marina and sometimes down to San Marcos Square. There you would meet with other families, play games, eat grilled corn on the cob or just listen to stories from the elders.

My Papa was such a gentleman. He always smelled of bay rum, never took up drink or smoke and wore a shirt, tie and hat as a proper businessman should. As he aged, he used a cane to walk, but I remember he always walked tall, even though he was only about 168 meters, five foot six. His face was gentle, always with a smile. His hair was cut close to his head and combed in a style that made you think of a studious person. He was an honorable man; at least this is what I have heard. I forgot to tell you what his occupation was, he was an accountant. He handled many accounts for farmers and fishermen that either didn't have the time to do their books or did not have the education. His desk was always full of papers and shelves upon shelves of books. He would say, 'this could be a library; however, the reading would not be particularly good for many.'

And Mama? Ah, she loved Papa! As I have said, she was up before him, and usually in bed after him. She was the core of the family, the one who brought order to our home. Not only did she cook, shop, clean, but she also made sure that the food was prepared whenever a special guest of Papa's would be entertained in our salon. She loved working with her hands, and would crochet doilies and tablecloths and sold them at a market nearby. Being only about 157 meters, five foot two, she seemed to tower over all of us; maybe it was how she wore her hair, up in a high bun, long dresses and of course a bit of heel on her boots. I remember her scent as that of roses. As I grew up, I asked her how she could afford the rose fragrance. She laughed, 'My darling, all you do is place rose petals into boiling water, let it boil for a while, then take it off the stove and let it set. Simple, but wonderful.'

She was always fresh and clean and never smelled like food. I told her this once, and she again just laughed, 'Such is many secrets you will learn as you grow into womanhood.'

Most of Mama's cooking was food for the body, but once in a while she would make a candy, maybe not candy, but a treat. Greeks generally don't eat much candy. This particular goody, I believe was taught to her from someone who had relatives in the Middle East, it's called Mhalabieh. She would take milk, sugar, rose water, corn flour, mystica (sprinkle just a bit) bringing it to a boil then pour it in small cups. Then she would put it in the coolest place in the house and once it set up, she would sprinkle it with cinnamon. She didn't make it too often, but when she did...what a treat! And, on special occasions Papa would bring home pastel which is made of sesame seeds and honey or mantolato which is made from egg whites, honey and almonds. Mama would say, 'we will have this treat, it is a very special treat, not good for every day.' At the end, all of the goodies would be gone. To this day I still treasure taking treats sparsely, but I love a good treat!

Ah, the love between my parents was real. Po po po, some as I heard thought it was an arranged marriage. Oh, no, it was out of love, as marriage should be. 'Friendship,' Mama said, 'is the basis of love. If you have a friend when you court, he will respect you through the hard times and good times, and when love waivers, your friend will always be there at your side'.

But their courtship was very difficult. You see, Mama was from the nobility. Nobility was the upper class of the island. I wonder if you are surprised that there is a class system? I think with any society there are those who have possessions and those that do not. And on Zakynthos, for generations there was the ruling class who owned much of the land and then there were the workers who at times owned some property but not like the nobility. Mama's family were farmers who owned much land. On the island it is said, 'a man who owns land is never poor.' So how did Mama, a woman from a wealthy family marry a man like Papa who was not of means? As I have said, it is a love story. When Papa was a young man he worked in the fields of Mama's family farm. With excellent grades and his work ethic, Papa progressed from field work to working in the office.

The farm raised currants, grapes for wine and olive trees for oil. Papa's position started as the trader to keep track of all transactions, and then onto being an accountant as I stated earlier. As he grew older, he went out on his own and started a co-op helping farmers with selling and transporting their goods.

Now that he was a business owner on his own, his status rose in the nobility's eyes; however, the one thing that Papa couldn't buy or obtain was being from nobility. And this caused problems.

Then how did they become a couple? Well, one thing that brought them together was that while he worked for Mama's family, Papa's office was in their home.

It was assumed that neither would associate with each other, but as days turned to weeks and then into months the family asked Mama to serve drinks at meetings and then, well shall we say, one thing led to another?

Mama said that she always felt that Papa was "the one", and as Papa would say, 'the one but don't touch!' They would laugh at this, but Papa was fairly accurate. As time passed and they started declaring their love, and Papus found out about their blooming relationship he tried many times to discourage it. 'You cannot marry below you,' he told Mama. 'You must find someone of your class.' 'Endaxi (okay),' she would say. Every time the subject was broached, she would declare her speech with 'endaxi,' never trying to make problems. However, she still worked hard at getting her father to see that Papa was a good man, nobility or not. Papous admitted that Papa was a good man and that he was capable of doing great things, but again the word 'nobility' or 'class' held him back on agreeing with their relationship.

Once Papa left Papous' farm and opened his own business, Papous started pulling back on his "stubbornness." That's what Mama called it; but it was more that the class structure was being broken. 'Let us see how Nionios does and then we shall talk.'

All the times before Papous would not even discuss the possibility of courtship, and now? Mama said, 'it was like a lightning bolt had hit her heart. There was the ray of hope that I had longed for. I now could wait until my last breath; the one person who was unmovable was changing ever so slightly but still moving!' Where was Yaya in all this? Ah, she knew her place, as all great women do. What is the saying, 'behind every great man stands a greater woman?' I believe that is why the mountain was even moving. So, over the next three years time ticked slowly but as grandmother said, 'Yes, it went slowly, but the clock never stopped.' When Papa asked for Mama's hand, Papous, with my Yaya at his side agreed.

It would take another two years before their marriage but what a wedding – what a celebration. And as the years grew so did my father's business.

My father wanted his business to provide for his family and, he never wanted to be bigger than others. 'This is Zakynthos, where living here is the dream we live with, not want for riches of money. Prosperity is when a family is good, just and a man finds them deserving. Ah, and that those who know us, will know we are a good family'. He would always conclude with Shalom.

Mama then moved out of her parent's house and into my father's world, his home where they melded their lives together.

It was almost a perfect fit. Even though Mama was nobility, she said to me, 'I like cooking, cleaning, working with my hands. Being part of the noble society you have people doing those things for you. I felt when I married your father that I received a decree that declared I could be myself and do things by and for myself. This was a day of great joy. First I received a good man as a husband and partner for life, and secondly, I received a chance to do what I wanted without my father telling me, "that is not what nobles do." Ah! I must not have been of noble blood as I didn't care what nobles did or didn't do. It was like an independence day for me, and I thank your father for this.'

She went about to make the apartment a home. She began to crochet tablecloths, new curtains and soon she discovered she was with child. Fortunately, her first was to be a boy. I know you must think, 'why is having a boy more important than a girl?' For a man to have the heir to his business and carry on his name is like giving him one of the greatest gifts. Mama felt proud that her first child was a male and that it was her gift back to her husband for everything he had given her.

Themesoticles (Themos for short) was received with much fanfare into Soula and Nionios' lives, as well as my Papous'. He was again like a small child with a toy. He made sure that everyone knew that he was a Papous- 'Grand Papa'.

And now my story, my life. Let me see, I was born in our home. My mama's sister who was also our next door neighbor assisted in my birth. I am told I was an easy birth and was smiling when I came into the world. This I do not know, as I have always heard that all babies are slapped and therefore they cry. But, I will allow the memory of my birth to be as it is, remembered fondly by all who were there.

As tradition, my name was not announced until my dedication one full year from my birth date. For a whole year, my name was bebe, that's right baby. Mama had thought long and hard about my name. Papa had decided on the first child a son, the first child using grandpa's name, so as tradition would have it, Mama could name me. So on my name date, or as you know it, birthday, in front of the family and friends, I was pronounced Anastasia Maria to everyone. Papa stood proud next to Mama whispering to her, 'Now, our family is complete. One boy, one girl, a full circle. As God has given, let no man put asunder. Amen. Shalom.'

He didn't know that as I was being dedicated another bebe was stirring in Mama's stomach! In 1931, Nikos was born. He broke the mold! Loud was his middle name. Papa would remark, 'we should have stopped with dia.' Mama would put her finger to her mouth, 'We are all equal. Some have louder voices that others. In time. In time,' as she rocked Nikos to quiet him down. I was beginning to walk, but with Themos' help we would run into our room, or out onto the veranda and cover our ears. 'It hurts too much.' Now look at him, a school teacher, keeping his mouth open even at the beginning. I laugh at this today, but I believe that my Papa only thought two children would be living in his household not three; but as such, Nikos arrived and the smile on my Papa's face was not any less broad than with his two other children. Mama used to say that three children under the age of five was very hard on her, but also rewarding. She said, 'I had a bigger bundle of joy all at once.' It always surprises me just how Mama kept a bright attitude. But knowing that this was the life she had always wanted makes more sense. It was an easy life with both of my parents. Their love spilled over to us. And I also believe that God being in the center of our family, he made the family one unit. As you entered and left the apartment, you acknowledged the blessings that were given and those that are to come. As my father left to go downstairs, you would hear the tapping of his koboloi beads. You may not have seen these, but they are also called worry beads. To me, they look like rosary beads, men hit them back and forth holding one end in their palm and the other end hitting the top of the hand; someone told me once that they thought they had been brought over from Turkey during the Ottoman invasion; this I do not know. But, most Greek men will have a pair and they will have them in their hands all day, every day.

I must tell you that there were several items that being a noble exposed to Mama that others were not, including a higher education. The nobility received not only the lessons of Greece, but also of Italy and France. Her knowledge seemed to know no bounds, and even today I want to run to her and ask her a question, knowing that she would have the answer that would make me ponder, but also have me reflect on. She loved to read, to know.

Since the public schools only taught Greek and of course now, English, Mama would teach me Italian and French. Themos would protest, 'Greek is our language!' Not listening to his protests, I begged to learn everything. Mama would say, 'why can't Themos be like you!' I would smile, 'oh Mama, he is like Papa.' She would smile, 'True. Even though he is two years older than you, age does not bring knowledge.'

Papa would tell Mama, 'someday he will become the man of the house, he needs to learn the simple things of life.' This conversation went on each time I asked something new. I miss those days. Ella.

At night, while Papa was in his shop or working on papers in the salon, Mama would come into our bedrooms and sing lullabies to help us sleep. Of course, my brothers didn't care for this as much as I. She would sit on the edge of my bed, stroking my hair, and she would sing, 'I give you my very young, bring them back to me grown up.' That is all I remember, as I would curl up into a bundle and fall fast asleep.

Denny, you have said many times, 'I feel so much love around you Nana.' I believe you feel the spirit of your grandparents, the foundation they instilled in me. May their souls find joy and happiness in heaven as they found on Earth. Shalom.

When my parents were married, my grandparents gave them almost four hectors of land in the area of the island close to Ag Pandes, which is in the village of Galaro. Papa was so proud of this land. On the Sundays that he could find time, we would go for our 'adventure' as Mama would say. Most roads were dirt, whereas in town the streets were cobblestone. There were no cars and very few buses which went from village to village. So, we would borrow a neighbor's mule drawn wagon for the day and climb aboard, and set out on our 'adventure'. There weren't many road signs so of course, and at times we would get lost. That didn't matter, Mama would lean into Papa and say, 'Was it this way or that? If you can't find the way to our new home, how can we find the way back to the town?' They would laugh and soon we would find our little place in the middle of the island.

Papa's 'dream land,' as Mama called it was actually the low land of the island almost exactly in the middle of the island. Farmers would farm this land, but not many would live there.

The wagon would rumble through vineyards and olive groves and all the while we'd listen to Papa tell stories of his hopes and dreams for the land. Never would we tire as if they were Papa's dreams then they were our families hopes and dreams too. It was Themos who would generally scream, 'Papa it's over there!' when the pine tree came into sight. 'Yes my son, once again we have made the journey and we are all well.'

Once there, a sheet would be spread out onto a clearing and bread, olives, cheese and the like would be served. A parasol was put up to protect our skin from the sun. During our early visits, Papa planted Mama a pinkish red rose. If it was blooming on our visits, she would take the blooming stems off and take them home to make her rose water. On the property there was an old Roman well and of course the pine tree that Papa would say, 'some day you all will grow big and strong as this tree.'

Mama picked up a pine cone one day and said, 'I have heard that if you watch a pine cone it will tell you the weather.'

Papa was appalled, 'Tee? (What) How can a little thing like that tell the weather?'

'When it is to rain, the hard outside will curl up, and when it is to be sun, they lie back down.'

Papa laughed, 'Take it home. But I will not sit around looking at a pine cone. I will look up at the sky. I know for sure that the clouds can tell me of rain or not. Or watch the fisherman, if they go out or stay in port, but a pine cone?' I cannot remember if it is true or not, but I do remember Mama putting several pine cones in the basket for safe passage for the journey home.

Denny, someday we must see if this is true, you do know where we can get some pine cones? Maybe they will predict the weather better than some on the nightly news does!

Signómi. (Sorry) I must tell you the rest of the story.

We didn't have many toys, but what we did have is our imaginations. And with the imagination of a child, games are invented. One of those games was chasing butterflies. Oh, the butterflies! They were everywhere. Different colors, shapes and sizes. We would chase them around the well, the tree, but never around Mama's rose bush. I cannot remember the family who had the property around ours, but they had planted olive trees and grape vines. In fact, Papa allowed them to plant some in the front part of our land. 'We do not have time to do it now, but it is best that someone use the land.'

We could only go out to the property in the late spring to early autumn, as when the rains came, it would be harder to take a wagon out onto the dirt roads, which by then were turning into mud. We knew Papa missed his land, but would say, 'we can wait. It will still be there even if we aren't there.'

For those hours that we 'lived' on the land, Papa would walk each inch of it. H would find stones and place them where the house's boundaries would be. Cruisina, saloni, krevatokamara and an ipnohomatio. Mama would ask, 'Banio?' 'Ohi,' Papa would cry out, 'Ohi, banio!' And then laugh, lean over and hug Mama.

What is a banio? It is a bathroom.

That's why I think they had a good marriage, they could tease each other. Ah, while Papa walked the land, Mama would put a watermelon, the cheese, any meat into the water bucket and lower it into the well. She would yell to Papa, 'ohi, banio?' Carrying a rock or clearing the weeds with the spade he would respond, 'ohi. ohi banio! Kala spiti!'

After several hours; after all the chasing of the butterflies, the moving of rocks, the clearing of the land and the food eaten, the watermelon was brought up from the well. Bravo! It was cool, sweet and messy. Papa made sure we would leave before the sun hit the western mountains. From the time it hit the mountains we knew we had just enough time to get onto the main roads and back into town.

And as we left, Papa would always face south and say, 'Grant us o Lord time to live on this land.' Shalom

We always wished that we could move to Papa's dream land, but that didn't even become a hint of reality until about 1954.

Our dwelling was a small, three bedroom apartment a couple blocks from the marina. The hustle and bustle of the middle part of town was exciting, but what I really loved was when the ferry horn would blow. I would run to the window and watch the smoke billow from the smoke stack, rising high in the sky. It happened about three times a week bringing visitors and supplies to the island. Papa, as well as others would lock up their shops and go down to the marina to either be enlisted in helping off load the cargo or gathering their orders to return to the mainland. The ferry would stay overnight and then head back to Patras the next morning, again blowing its horn with plumes of smoke billowing out of the smoke stack. As I grew older, Papa would take us down with him on occasion. The ship was enormous and the excitement could hardly be contained. When we got back to the apartment, he would sit down with Mama and tell her the news from Athens and beyond.

I keep trying to remember any bad times; however, all I can remember is a peace in our house. Oh, there had to be hard times, but I never heard either of my parents raise their voice; argue, nothing. Was this an ideal home? No, but when it came to family life, my parents closed their door to discuss. That is one thing I brought into my marriage too, no one else should know your business.

My childhood was filled not only with a good family life, but also with a lot of celebrations. I believe all people like to celebrate and Greeks are not to be outdone!

Let me see, the year starts off with a day to honor St. Vassilis. Who is this St. Vassilis? I laugh now, but to be honest it's St. Nicholas or Santa Claus! Ne. When I was young he was celebrated on New Year's Eve not on the 25th day of December. No tree was placed in his honor, but a cake was baked, then divided up. Mama would bake a cake called St. Vassilis's cake or Vasilopitta. On New Year's Eve, all friends and relatives are invited to your home and then when the clock strikes midnight, the lights are turned off and then back on again, to mark the end of the old year and the beginning of the new. Then the cake, the Vasilopiita was cut. The cutting of the cake is where the excitement truly begins. For, a single gold coin was baked into the cake. Whoever finds the coin, so custom says, will have good luck for the whole year. When the cake is cut, the first piece is cut in honor of the Virgin Mary, the second is for the father of the family and the third for the mother, and so on. Who gets the piece cut for the Virgin Mary? It is taken out into the streets and given to a needy person of the neighborhood.

Also, tradition has it that pomegranates should be placed outside the front door or over the fireplace to bring luck for the upcoming year. Ne, that messy, many seeded fruit is a symbol of good fortune, good luck.

Ah, then there's the 6th of January, the day is called Epiphany, 'the blessings of the waters.' This day is to celebrate the baptism of Jesus by St John. Throughout our country crosses are thrown into the sea, lakes and rivers, then brave swimmers dive into the water to retrieve the crosses.

The second half of February is carnival season or the Apokrias. It lasts until 'Clean Monday'. Young and old dress up hold parades. February was also Papa's name day month (birthday). Exactly 40 days before Easter is 'Clean Monday', the beginning of Lent; tradition has it that you should go out and fly a kite, and eat a traditional fasting meal.

March was Nikos' name day and on the 25th is one of the major Greek national holidays; the day commemorating the Greek victory over Turkey ending the War of Independence.

Greek Orthodox Easter is in April or early May. Sometimes, my name day and Easter fell were on same day. Easter is a week of celebrations. It is called Andetia, where church services can be heard from one end of the town to the other. The church bell towers would ring out loud the glory of the day. We did not participate in every aspect of the Easter celebration, but what is exciting is that on the day called Holy Saturday is the breaking of jugs. This is an old custom from ancient time, I believe it started in Corfu, or it could even be from the Venetians; anyway, if you fill a jug full of water, and throw it off your balcony it will exorcise evil. Early that morning, the Philharmonics go around in the streets, playing joyful tunes while people throw and *break clay pots outside their houses. And then at sunrise, from the town of Aghios Nicolaos, the Bishop would ring the church bells and set white pigeons free in the air. On Easter Sunday, a solemn procession takes place when the Byzantine icon of the Holy Mother of Chryssopigi is carried around the city streets up to San Marco square, where at midnight the Bishop with a candle gives life to a chain of candles that multiply to enlighten the whole square. Ah, two important things happen during this time, lambs are roasted in the square as people folk dance as well as the presentation of the red eggs. Ne, eggs are painted red are either displayed by themselves or baked in bread. Why? I suppose to indicate the blood of Christ. But, one legend has it that an old woman did not believe in this man, Jesus. So, as she went to her hen house to gather eggs, lo and behold there was a bundle of eggs, all in red. They say, she then believed. A miracle or a myth? Who knows, but certain traditions like the red eggs and the throwing of the jugs made festive and fun.*

Another custom I like very much is a game for the young and old. You hold a red egg in your hand and another person has one in theirs. They greet you with the words, "Christos Aneste" (Christ is Risen); then you answer "Alethos Aneste" (Truly, He is Risen). Then your friend strikes your egg with the pointed end of theirs. The person whose egg manages to remain uncracked is the winner. It is very hard to have an uncracked egg! And, thank goodness the eggs are hardboiled!

    Papa says it is okay if we participate a little. Just so we are not getting caught up in the religious aspect of the celebration. I am laughing now, because also, the young boys on the island would go in the late Saturday evenings when the businesses were all closed, go around and gather the hanging business signs and put some in the square or they would put them all around town on different businesses. The hardware store on Easter morning would be the Pharmacia! No one got mad and the boys had a lot of fun. This also gave the business people of Zakynthos town a chance to meet, swap stories...I suppose you couldn't do that anymore?

    On the fifteenth day of August is the celebration for the Virgin Mary. Oh, and I forgot, someone changed this to the twenty sixth day of August because it attracted more tourists, ohi it was probably because of the earthquake, ne, the final day of the earthquake. Originally it was on the seventeenth day of December (in my heart that is still the day) it is the day to celebrate the patron saint of the island. Papa would remind us, 'we only participate with this ceremony as he is the saint of this island and must be remembered'. Aglos (Saint) Dionysios' preserved body is brought out and taken through the streets, believing that this will bless the island for one more year. I still shake my head at why he is a saint, but then again, I am not one to judge. It is said that the reason he obtained sainthood is that as a monk he stayed at the Monastery of Anafonitria he heard a knock, opened the door and magnanimously gave shelter to the assassin of his brother who was being chased by the Turks. He hid his own brother's murderer and then later helped him escape the island. I suppose there were other items that added up to saint hood, but...I wander, signómi.

Mama's and Themos' name days were celebrated together in September and on the 28th of October is 'Ohi Day', celebrating the fact that the Greeks stood up the Italians and said NO at the beginning of the Second World War.

As you can see, there are a lot of celebrations in Greece, but mainly we have always celebrated our family. Mama would say, 'the main thing we must remember is that we are together and that is what we celebrate more than anything else.'

Our lives were simple and oh, how I enjoyed living on Zakynthos. That all changed in 1943. In the middle of the night there was a knock at the door. Papa grabbed his outer wrap and greeted a visitor at the shop door. 'You must take your family and simple possessions with me now.' Papa tried to argue, but the man was insistent. Mama was not willing to go with such confusion, but the look on Papa's face was enough for her to concede. We were pulled from our beds, and asked to dress quickly. Mama said, 'take your school books and your dolly.' I, being eleven at the time wanted more answers, but when I looked at her, 'nothing else?' There was only one reply, 'nothing else'.

Then she went to get Nikos and Themos up. In a matter of minutes we were rushing down the staircase and into a mule drawn wagon.

'You must lie as close to the floor of the wagon as possible,' This man said as he lifted us one by one into the wagon. 'I must do this for your safety.' And that was when a tarp was placed over us and then what sounded like rain, but what was straw was piled onto top of the tarp. He whispered into the side of the wagon, 'Keep your heads down and stay under the tarp, no matter what happens.' As we snuggled next to each other Papa spoke softly, 'do not speak, not even a whisper until we are safe. Not one word.'

Under the tarp it was dark, but after awhile my eyes began to adjust. I could make out Mama somewhat, as I sat next to her, I also felt her as she gently rocked back and forth. I leaned into her and slowly, her arm reached around me, a hint of roses made my head spin, with her I was safe. I wanted to cry, wanted to talk, wanted to scream-but knowing of the warning I closed my eyes with so many thoughts running through my mind. Without seeing him, I knew that Papa was holding onto his koboloi beads tightly-but not a sound came from them. On each side of him, he held both Nikos and Themos, 'Let us be brave and pray for safety.' Were the last words spoken.

As we snuggled close together trying to not even breath, the feeling of danger, that something was terribly wrong crept into our beings.

What was happening to our world? Why were we being driven from our home? Especially in the dead of night and in a wagon with a tarp over us, being smuggled like bandits?

Papa was always a proud man who was one not to hide anything; but this time he too was in hiding. What was happening?

The further we traveled and the silence that surrounded us and adding the feeling I received from

Mama's body told me what Papa had always said, 'little girls like you ask too many questions.' But one thing was clear, we were in grave danger. But why? My heart started beating faster. Had Themos or Nikos done something wrong and now we were paying for it by hiding under a layer of tarp and hay? If this is so...my mind wandered through the past days trying to figure out the true meaning of all this.

The road grew bumpy as the wagon left the streets of the town and onto the country roads. A couple of times the cart stopped, we heard muffled voices which may have been the driver talking to someone. But the language wasn't familiar. Hearing the voices, fear grew and hands were being grabbed and held tight. We lay as still as we could under the tarp and hay.

Time felt stale. Minutes ticked slowly. Suddenly we heard our driver's voice yell, 'Ella!' and the wagon thrust forward.

Many times it felt like the wagon was going to break in two as it hit the ruts or a ditch on the side of the road. Other times it felt like it was going to break in two as it swayed back and forth and bumped up and down. With all this turbulence the wagon never once failed us, nor our driver.

The twists and turns in the road, the climbing up and down hills seemed like hours. I must have fallen asleep because I was startled when the wagon stopped and the tarp flew open. 'Go quickly and be very silent.' Nikos and Themos jumped out of the cart and helped Mama, Papa and myself out. I looked up, we had came to Aghios Georgios Monastery of Gremnon! So far away from home, why?

Once inside we were told the news. A man dressed as a priest, began to describe in detail what was happening. 'The Germans had seized the island and that they were ordered to round up all of the "undesirables".'

We were undesirables, but how? Wasn't Papa a well respected businessman? And what did his family do? Mama stayed home and his three children just went to school. Then it hit me. In San Solomos Square there was a large flag, no banner with a symbol that looked like a cross with bent angles, what did Papa call it? A...it's a strange word, a swastika! I almost screamed it, but nothing came out. That's it! The Nazi army was taking over the island and we needed to hide. But again, why us?

The German army (the Nazis) stationed themselves in Zakynthos town by the marina, and also inland at Katastari as well as other key points. Why the road through Katastari? Ah, it was the only main road (dirt as it was) to the northern part of the island as well as the road to Ag. Nikolaos which was the harbor for ships to go to and from Kephalonia.

The man dressed as a priest also stated that the German army was asking for all of those of the Jewish faith to be turned over so that Hitler could have them transported to a concentration camp.

Under my breath I said, 'we're undesirable… Jews?'

'Papa, are we Jewish?' Themos asked.

This was the first time we had heard about this. We knew that Papa didn't hold the same values as others on the island, but we did not know we were of the Jewish faith.

'Ah, it is not only a faith, but also a heritage. We are first and foremost Greek, your ancestors are Jewish and therefore, so are we.'

We were shown to small rooms without heat. Mama slept with me, Papa had the boys sleep together and Papa left us alone. When he did come back it was morning to wake us up. 'The wonders of this God, I do not know.'

Mama took his hand, 'Tell us.'

Papa looked worn, but bent his head a bit and said, 'It is said that the Nazis have asked for all the names of all those of the Jewish faith to be turned over to them by tomorrow morning.'

Mama exclaimed, "But we are not of that faith!"

'In the eyes of those men, we are. If it wasn't for the fast thinking of the Mayor and the Bishop, we would be on that list. But, they felt that we were in grave danger and helped us escape.'

Themos asked, 'Because we were born a Jew?'

'Ne.'

What we soon learned was that the day before our 'escape into the hills,' the Nazis in command went to see the Mayor and the Bishop of the island. 'You will give us all the names of all the Jews on the island.'

The Mayor asked if he and the Bishop could have some time to gather the names. 'Why what have they done?'

'We are commanded by our leader, Mein Hitler, to gather all of these that will not assist us to further the cause of Nazi Germany.'

'But surely, not on our island.'

'They are everywhere and must be placed for detainment, rounded up so that we know where they are at all times.'

The Mayor tried to find the words. As he listened to the German officer standing in front of him he felt a shiver going down his spine; to be detained and killed. He didn't know if that was true, but the blood curdling feeling he received from the officer was enough for him. Choosing his words slowly and precisely he hoped this would be enough, 'We have never thought of who was of one religion or ethnic background or the other. To us we are all Greek.'

The commander agreed, 'We give you 24 hours.'

The Mayor looked at the Bishop and then back to the officer, 'Only 24 hours? This does not give us enough time.'

'It is all the time you have, use it wisely.'
When the military left, a decision was made almost on the spot that, 'We cannot, under any circumstance turn anyone over to these barbarians. These are our people and we were chosen to protect them.'

'Protect we will.'

The Mayor then dispatched some his most trusted men to go and work out a plan with the businessmen on how to protect all of the Jewish people. Once they heard what was happening it was unanimous what was to be done.

So, trying to outguess the German army, some went to the two synagogues and talked to the Rabbis and others to farmers.

'Why have you come to this house of God? We have not seen your faces pass through these doorways ever.'

Quickly and as precisely as they could, they were told of what was happening on the island.

'This cannot be? How could this be happening on our beloved Zante? What have our people done?'

The discussion was frenzied. With talk about the various reports which had come from Germany, Poland, even as close as Kephalonia they knew it was more true that they had wished.

Immediately they entrusted the leaders with all 275 names.

'Go with God. Have mercy on us all.'

One of the leaders spoke out, 'Are you not Jewish too?'

'Ne we are.'

'Then you are to be protected as well.'

'What would they want with us.'

'If you do not come, you will be transported off the island and taken possibly to Germany. And from

reports we have heard you will not be heard from again.'

'Then come back for us, we will spend the day making it look like our synagogues are like museums as well as taking all our personal possessions. If they do come for us, they will only find a very clean house of God.'

As the sun set, the leaders' plan was about to be enacted, secretly, using the list from the Rabbis. They went to each and every home gathering up everyone and smuggling them into the night. Many were, like us, placed in wagons with tarp and hay on top. Did it not look strange that local farmers hauling their hay to various parts of the island in the late evening hours or early morning? Fortunately, the Nazis were only patrolling heavily during the day and did not become wise to what was happening.

Precisely twenty-four hours later the military were at the steps of the Mayor's office. Standing side by side and in agreement were the Mayor and the Bishop. Proudly, the Mayor handed the officer a sheet of paper with all the names of those of the Jewish faith.

But once the list was read, the Nazi Commander was outraged, 'Only two?'

'Ne. Bishop Chrysostomos and myself, Pavios Carreris. 'said the Mayor.

'I was told there were to be more.' As he turned he looked at the Bishop, who was all dressed in his black robe and hat, 'You are not Jewish. I demand to see their businesses.'

So, off they went to the business district. What had been decided was that a business day would be like any other with all the business would open on time with the Jewish owned shops being run by other shop keepers who were 'acting' like they owned the shops. Ne, the merchants went into the Jewish business, open the doors, putting out the wares – copper, brooms, jewelry then stood in the doorways as the Nazis came to inspect the businesses. After going through several shops, the officer with much disgust shoved the list back into the Mayor's hands and ordered his men to patrol the streets. 'They will come back, and when they do we will be waiting for them.'

However, within weeks the war had turned badly against them, and the Nazis posted on Zakynthos left and went to Kephalonia or back to Germany and some to Italy. We were spared, all of us. Ah, the people of the island, all the faiths bound together to help each other. Bravo! When we were allowed to return home, we rode home in the cart but this time on top of the hay.

    Trying to put our lives back as before was not easy. For many weeks Papa was always making sure that he or Mama went everywhere with us. And then, we too looked around as nothing seemed to be the same. Maybe it was that people knew we were Jewish or now that we knew but there seemed to be a difference in the air. We didn't understand the fullness of the actions by our fellow islanders until much later when we found out what happened in the concentration camps, and how truly our lives had been spared by that one single act by the Mayor and the Bishop, our love for the people of Zakynthos grew even more. No one ever stated that the portion of town where the Jewish people lived and operated their businesses was called the 'Jewish Quarter.' I say this now, because to me, I never felt that there was a separation or difference.

    Time did pass and things fell back in place. Papa's business seemed to continue without harm, but I did notice that Mama continued to watch us all more carefully. She would say, 'Anna, where do you go?' I say, 'out to the street to play in the square.' 'Parakaló, stay close.'

Ah, and Kephalonia? It was said that the island was occupied by both the Italians some say added up to about 12,000 men and about 2,000 Nazi Germans, for a while they cohabitated on the island together for the same cause, communism. When the armistice with Italy was agreed upon in September of 43 things became chaotic. The Italians decided to return back to their homeland. Ships were loaded and many Italian soldiers left. However during their departure, the Nazi Germans felt that the ammunitions should remain. The Italians stated that this was too much to leave and therefore the two forces that were once friendly found themselves at a stalemate. The Germans voted to fight and the Italians passed a referendum among the soldiers to choose either surrender or fight.

They fought. The Italians held out for around six hours; however, the Germans prevailed, taking full control of the whole island. Of the remaining 6,000 surviving Italian soldiers, they were brutally rounded up and executed by the Nazis. Once the massacre had taken place, the Germans eventually left the island.

With our islands so close to each other, we on Zante were fortunately the horrors of what took place on Kephalonia.

In 1947 or 1948 Themos left to serve the Greek army as it was mandatory for every young man after graduation to serve. And because of what had happened to us and the Nazis, Themos was proud to serve. Papa was proud to have <u>his son</u> be part of this nation and country called Greece. He looked so handsome in his uniform and as we all went down to the marina to see him board the ship bound for Piraeus, Mama started to cry. Themos, kissed her on both cheeks and said, 'Mama, I am grown up now. I do this for all of Greece.' Mama hugged him and said, 'You are my first and always will be. Come home safe.' We stayed until the ferry left the harbor, billowing its dark smoke into the sky, waving and throwing kisses until we could no longer see the ferry. He left a boy of sixteen and, no matter what he had to face, the next time we would see him. He would surely be a man.

With Themos gone, Nikos and I became closer. It was nice to have the extra micro of space that Themos had taken up. Ah and how my dear brother Nikos loved to tease me; hiding my books, my shawl, other things that I would at that precise moment want but could not find. My patience would wear thin until Mama would turn and say, 'It is good that Nikos is still here, daxi?'

Throughout my school years, I had always been proud of my discipline. 'Education,' Papa would say, 'is what will help you through life'. Taking that to heart, I never had problems getting decent grades in school as I passed all my studies. But I was not ready for what was waiting for me while at school which was a boy or should I say a young man. He was taller than Papa, with dark hair and always a dark shadow of hair on his face. He would say, 'I have shaved, but it never goes away.' He was handsome with strong arms and a nice smile, but not of the Jewish faith. Now, please understand there weren't that many Jews on the island, something like 275. So, how was I to find a husband when most were already taken or were my brothers? Signómi. This was a point of discourse between Papa and I many times. Who won? Nobody, but it was surely me that lost.

Dionysios Stamaras, a good Greek Orthodox man was whom I had fallen in love with. There were many talks with Papa, Mama quietly sitting there between the two of us on 'How this was not right, look at Mama and myself and how we found each other.' 'How you will not find the happiness that our God wants for you?' 'How, bringing Dionysios into a Jewish home was wrong.' However, with mamma's help, it was decided that we could see each other. 'With his presence here or you at his parents, that is it.'

Slowly our dates were not at either parents' home, but in the park, the square, up at the old fort, down at the red rock and on the beach. I knew that I had found someone to love, who like Papa for Mama, was a very good person. I never voiced this to him, or to Mama nor Papa, but when your heart tells you these things, you must listen. Love, agape love, only happens once in your life, if you are lucky. It's not butterflies or giddiness, yes that happens also, but it's the knowledge that you have a friend whom you trust and have a bond with.

The last year of school was coming to a close, and with me being almost eighteen and he close to twenty the inevitable was to be faced, he signed the papers in which to serve in the army just like Themos.

He looked good in his uniform, smiling and kidding me he said, 'Ne, I look good except...' and we both said it together, 'the whiskers on your face.' His face leaned into mine and we shared a kiss that was so different from before, as I felt like we had melded into one. He held me close and whispered in my ear, 'S'agapó.'

I stood still. I had waited so long to hear that word. 'S'agapó.' It rang in my ears, in my heart and in my mind. Dionysios loved me. He pulled back, placing something into my palm and rolling my fingers over it, 'always.' I didn't know where to look, in his eyes, in my hand but once I collected my thoughts I did both. His eyes were the darkest brown and filled with tears. I stood on my toes to kiss them ever so gently and then I opened my hand. Staring back at me was a ring, 'It is proper, it is right. I know of no other to have to share my life with.'

As time grew closer to Dionysios' departure we knew that we couldn't hold onto our decision alone. But, how was the best way to break the news, a Gentile and Jew were engaged, and without their families' blessings. As tradition would have it, Dionysios should have gone to Papa first to ask for my hand, <u>then</u> come to me. I started to get worried and shared my fears with Dionysios. 'I will go to your father now and ask. Please do not tell anyone of our decision, and act surprised when I come to you with your father's blessing. And...'

Taking the ring out of the small pouch Dionysios gave me, I handed the gift back to him, 'and the ring cannot be seen until you ask my hand in marriage, please then return it to me properly.'

He smiled and accepting the pouch he wrapped his arms around me, 'your wish is my command.'

'You don't think...'

With his mouth pressed to mine, I never got to finish my sentence. 'Wish me luck.' And off he went down the stairs.

Mama entered the room and stood with her arms folded, 'it is about time he asked permission.'

'How did you know?'

'How could we not know.'

'We?'

'Ne. Your father and I have seen the glow on your face for weeks. And...'

'And, what? Mama, please. This might mean that Papa will not allow us to be married.' Just then I stopped. I had said it. Now look what I have done!

She let out a big laugh. 'So it is true.'

I sat down and started to cry. 'I truly love him.'

With her arms around me she sat down and spoke gently, 'the problem is that he is not Jewish.'

As I was about to speak, Mama interrupted me, 'but, he has taken your heart and made it full, it will work out.'

'It sounds like Papa and you have discussed this?'

'Since the moment you were born. Ne, it is true that we didn't expect it to be a Gentile, but he loves you that is apparent, so then we will make this work. He is down in the shop right now with your father, let us see how he handles himself. Papa has a lot of respect for Dionysios; so let us allow the men in our lives to work this out.'

Mama asked us to do it on a Tuesday afternoon. The town would be quiet and it would be more proper. We did. We waited.

When late afternoon came, Mama and I stayed upstairs waiting for Dionysios to make a proper call on Papa.

We sat on the steps with the door slightly cracked. The clock ticked, my heart pounded, and my thoughts ran rampant as I waited. And waited we did, but there was no sign of Dionysios. Soon, Mama got up and began busying herself in the kitchen fixing a lunchtime meal for Papa. I couldn't bear just waiting, hearing the clock ticking so I, too, went to the kitchen helping where I could. As I squeezed each lemon I became more and more calm, my thoughts wandered to almost a dreamlike state. Someday, I too will probably have a daughter who will be facing a similar decision and I will be making Dionysios his lunch while he is talking to our daughter's gentleman caller. Without knowing, I let out a large laugh.

'Daughter, is there something I should be let in on?'

I ran over and hugged Mama, 'no, just that everything will be okay. And that I am fortunate to have been born into this family.'

'I think the lemons have gone to your head.'

'Maybe they have.'

Just then we both turned, Mama whispered, 'was that a knock?'

I couldn't contain myself, 'He's here.'

'Hush child, he will hear us.'

'From up here?'

There were muffled voices from downstairs for what seemed like just a minute, and then a door slammed and quiet.

Forgetting myself, I ran past Mama, down the stairs and stopped when Papa said, "Dionysios has gone!'

I knew that I should not ask, but my heart was anxious and without thinking asked, 'gone?'

'As I said, he has left.'

'But why, may I ask?'

'My child, you need to sit.'

'I am almost a grown woman, I shall stand.'

'As you wish.' Papa walked over to the door, closing it slightly. 'You knew he was here?'

'Ne. I was upstairs with Mama preparing food when we heard voices down here.'

'And you knew it was your Dionysios?'

My words would not come.

'Come, my daughter. You ran down the stairs with fear in your footsteps, you must have hoped that it was his voice mixed with mine that filled this very room.'

'Papa, I mean no disrespect...'

'Then, what you say will not be taken as such.'

'It was Dionysios that was here with you, am I correct?'

'Ne.'

'And that he has come to talk to you about us, our future?'

'Ne.'

'And that you turned him away?'

Choosing his words carefully, he replied slowly, 'and if that is the truth?'

'Do you not think he is worthy?'

Papa began to laugh. Not a loud laugh, but one that grew from the belly and out into the air. 'Ne. He is worthy. I would very much like him to be part of this family.'

'And?'

'I asked him to do one thing that he must be prepared to answer before anything else.'

'Forgive me for being so bold to ask, but what is that?'

Papa walked up me and reached for my hand. I felt love in his touch, but also concern. 'A question that all fathers, ne, all parents wish for their future in laws to have, I asked him "What is your trade?" I cannot have my only daughter marry a Greek or anyone else for that matter whom does not have a trade.' With that, he then passed me and walked up the stairs.

Without hesitation, I threw open the door and ran out into the street. There was no Dionysios.

No sooner had I ran up the stairs and into my room than Papa called for me, 'Anna!'

Slowly making my way into the kitchen I found both Mama and Papa waiting for me. 'Anna, please, sit.' Mama's voice was stern but gentle, so pulling the chair out I sat and folded my hands into my lap.

'Papa, I am sorry for how I sounded just then. I wanted Dionysios so much to find grace in your eyes.'

Papa leaned over and placed his hands onto the table, 'my dearest, you have much to learn. I am not angry with Dionysios or even upset a little. I have asked him for something that any father would ask of a young man who is to ask for his daughter in marriage. Ne, Dionysios is from a fine family, I know them well. I have known Dionysios since God brought him to this world. I have seen him play, grow into a young man, and now he works very hard for his father. That said, I want to know what <u>his</u> future holds for him. He may stay with his father's business or do something else. My responsibility to you, to your mother and to our family is to make sure that he can provide for you and not just for you two, but also for any children you both might have. Fortunately for you, he has taken that to heart and gone to decide.'

Mama smiled to Papa and said, 'daughter, passion of the heart is just the beginning of the potion that stirs one's feelings into love. With love, you find commitment and a life together. But that does not provide the daily needs of a home. Your father is a good man, with a kind heart. He asks with courage that Dionysios will be back, and have the answer.'

That night, I went to bed earlier than usual, all the while in thought that maybe Dionysios would give up. My dreams kept haunting my thoughts, telling me that even though he knew in his heart we were to be one, he couldn't battle my father. Battle my father, for what? The next morning, I woke up as tired as I had lain down.

As I entered the living room, there stood Dionysios. 'Oh, I had not heard you come in.'

Papa turned to me, 'daughter, Dionysios and I were discussing something that is weighing heavy on his heart. Do you want to stay or leave to go back into your room?'

'I will stay.'

Dionysios bowed and continued, 'I am an honest man, yes a Greek, and honest never the less.'

Keeping to myself, I heard my mind say, 'I know Papa did not think that Greek men were either dishonest or lazy'.

'Sir after our talk yesterday I need to ask you something more before I ponder your question.'

'Parakaló.'

'While I am not of your faith. Will you still consider me once I tell you of my future position? Or, with respect, is this a way to have me retreat?'

I could tell that Papa was a bit taken aback. The conversation of faith had not truly been addressed, at least not out in the open.

'I asked you yesterday about your future and now we talk about our faiths. I respect one man's faith if his thoughts are that of God. I do not consider that one item to cement my daughter's hand in marriage. I am not the judge of one's faith. I am though, permitted by God to judge when it comes to being able to provide for my daughter's future.'

'Efharisto.' He stood up, shook my father's hand and stated, 'I love your daughter and know we are to be together. We will not see each other until I have an answer, and that answer will come soon.' He then turned to me, 'You will wait for me?'

My face must have had the look of surprise, 'Why do you ask? You know my answer.'

'As I cannot call upon you until an answer is given.'

'You know my answer.'

He then turned to Papa, 'Parakaló I hope that with my answer, you then will find it in your heart to allow marriage between your daughter and myself.'

Papa nodded, 'I will try.'

And with that, Dionysios turned, smiled at me, then went down the stairs.

When it was just the two of us in the room, Papa turned to me, 'I like him, ohi I like him very much.'

As he turned to head downstairs, I asked a question, 'does it matter about religion?'

'Not as much.'

'You found Mama, you are happy?'

'Ne,' he said, 'but we are of one faith. Happiness must be in your heart, if with one religion or two.'

'Ne,' I said, 'and with that you are one for eternity, so will Dionysios and I be.'

What was important to my father was balance. He had always brought that to our lives and now he was bringing it to my future. I looked up and noticed the clock on the wall. 'So, our time to wait starts now does it?' All it did was reply with a resounding tick.

Life seemed to continue as I waited. Chores were to be done. Mama took on the task of showing me how to do things such as embroidery, and darning socks and Papa asked me more and more to be with him down in the shop. He had me take the large books, ledgers and help him add up the figures, write invoices and ensure that I was kept busy. There were days when I was asked to run errands, help a distant relative and even assist in things outside Zakynthos Town. But the busier I was being kept, the more anxious my heart was to know Dionysios' answer.

A month passed before Dionysios appeared back at our house. I had gone to run an errand, and when I returned there he sat across the table from Papa. At first I did not see them together. I was so anxious to tell Papa something that had been told to me that when I entered the shop I nearly spoke out of turn, until I heard my Papa's voice, 'I believe you have chosen well. And so, you finally may ask. Ah, my daughter arrives.'

They both stood and Dionysios smiled, 'If I may, I would like to ask your permission to offer my hand in marriage to your daughter.'

Papa walked around the table and over to me, I bowed my head as he kissed both my cheeks. 'You're my only daughter and I want only the best for you. Your heart has chosen well.'

I looked into Papa's eyes; they danced with joy. He was well pleased. He took my hand and placed it into Dionysios'. 'You have both my blessing and that of my wife's.'

The stairway door flew open and out came Mama, running down the stairs and over to the both of us, crying and mumbling words of praise and thanksgiving.

Papa spoke with great conviction, 'We are blessed to have you join our home; however, you also must talk to your parents, and if they agree, then we will all be a family. Jew, Gentile, we are all God's children and should live as one.' With that he embraced me. Ever since I was a little girl, I loved being wrapped in my father's arms; the strength of his hug, the smell of his hair that of bay rum and the stillness of his breathing, my Papa was like home.

Papa reached his hand out to Dionysios, 'Welcome to our family.' As Dionysios took Papa's hand, he was pulled into the embrace. This surprised me immensely. Papa was not known for showing so much affection. It also dawned on me that Papa's voice had a quiver in it.

Finally we hugged as a newly engaged couple. I could feel my future husband's heart beat loudly. He whispered in my ear, 'agapi mou, agapi mou.'

As we pulled away, Dionysios stood a bit taller and straightened his clothes, 'I am to go now and inform my family. Thank you for welcoming me into your lives.' He smiled at me and as he was departing turned and said, 'Never have I known such joy.' As the door closed Mama ran over to me, 'Daughter, you are now grown to be a woman, where is my little girl?'

'Right here, Mama; as I will always be, right here.'

Papa excused himself to go back to work.

'Papa?'

'Yes, my daughter.'

'S'agapó.'

A smile crossed his face, showing his teeth, and replied, 'Ne. S'agapó.'

Mama's arms were around me as we walked up the stairs and as she led me to the couch. 'Now we wait.'

It didn't take long before Papa's voice called from the shop, 'Ella! Family, come quickly.'

As Mama and I ran down the stairs, we were startled to see Dionysios' parents near the front doorway.

Dionysios' father, who in my eyes was the grandest looking man in all the world, next to Dionysios I mean, held out his arms, 'Come daughter, it is agreed. Two families such as ours shall be joined as one. This is the way it should be.'

Mama clapped her hands.

Just then Themos walked into the shop. 'Te?'

I stepped forward, 'I am to be married to Dionysios.'

'Then it is true.' He kissed my cheeks and went over to Mama and put his arm around her shoulder, 'There will be more room in the apartment for us when she is gone.'

'Themos!' Mama exclaimed.

'I tease, but I do not lie. Congratulations Anna and Dionysios, we have been waiting a long time for this.'

With that I entered into a warm embrace with Dionysios father.

In what seemed like only a second, bottles of wine were brought out and cheers were pouring not only out of Papa's shop but up and down the streets.

My nights, days, hours and minutes were filled with, 'When are you going to get married?' 'What will you wear?' 'Where will it be?'

Those answers and others would all come fast enough, but first Dionysios had to do what all men of Greece did, and that was to serve his country.

I did not realize, but he had been called many months earlier, but he kept it quiet from me so that I would not have red eyes as he would call it. 'Tears are not becoming to an engaged woman. Some people will think that things are wrong if there are red eyes.'

'But would it also not be from joy?'

'Ne, joy, but when the ship takes your beloved away, joy is not the word you will be thinking about.'

'Ohi, I will be counting the days for your return.'

'Days? My dearest, days are not counted, but months.'

'I know, but days are easier to say…months sound long and then red eyes you shall always see.'

Dionysios laughed, 'I cannot wait to be your husband. My mama has always wanted a daughter and now she shall have one.'

'And a daughter I will be to her. Do not worry, I will be with her often while you are away.'

'I would hope so. She is wanting to discuss many things, details of our wedding, where we shall live, what you shall be wearing…'

'But Mama will also needed to be at these meetings…'

'Let us not call them meetings, but gatherings of the two families.'

'As you wish.'

'My true wish is that you will always be, as you are now.'

'You do see me growing up, too, do you not?'

'Ne. What I meant to say is that I want you to always be filled with love and a person that wants to live life. Always.'

'I owe that to my parents. They have never shown anything but kindness to others. That, I am certain I can also bring to our home.'

Just then, our lips met. I felt nothing but warmth and wholeness with him. His arms around my waist, my lips against his. Right then I knew what Mama must have felt when she is with Papa, complete.

There were many questions that were asked, but the main was, 'where will you two live?' I knew that when I was married to Dionysios, we would have a home somewhere. This brought other thoughts to my head, what about furniture? Curtains? Linens? Dishes? And what was I to do when we were married. I had lived my whole life within these walls which my parents had provided and never had I contemplated life outside them. And now, that was what I was being asked to consider. I wanted to ask Dionysios before he left, but I knew that he had too many things on his mind; and I couldn't ask his parents as they would think I was too pushy 'she's not even married yet and she wants to take control.' I can hear it now, and what about

Mama...would she understand? So, I decided to stay quiet, 'it will all work out. This I what I have to believe.'

On the day of his departure we all stood on the dock; our parents, Dionysios and myself. Dionysios in his uniform stood proud and when his father stretched out his hand, Dionysios saluted him. His father leaned in and embraced him. 'My son, come home safe.'

'I intend to, father; I have a wonderful future to look forward to; He whispered and then, pulling back hugged his mother and then it was myself. He took me into his arms and said, 'I know we have never kissed in public before,' with that his body engulfed mine and as our lips parted I knew I was truly in love.

'Come home soon.'

'I shall.'

'Nineteen months is a very long time.'

'Believe me. It will go by slowly but also very fast.' He then put my chin into his palm. 'You are the only one that has my heart.'

'And mine yours.'

Just then the whistle on the steam ship blew and he kissed me again, quickly, slipping something into my pocket he whispered, 'do not look at it until you no longer see the ship. Daxi?'

Tears started falling from my eyes down onto my cheeks, 'Daxi.'

'Remember, no red eyes.'

I tried as hard as I could to pull them back and wipe them away with my hands. 'I will try, no red eyes.'

He turned, picked up his knapsack and ran to the ship, half turning as he ran waiving and screaming, 'S'agapó! S'agapó!'

Before I knew it, he was on the ship, Mama and Papa were next to me and the ship was treading water to leave.

We stood watching the ship slowly cross the bar and head out onto the open sea. When the ship could no longer be seen, I reached into my pocket. Feeling around I found a little pouch, and drawing it open I found a necklace - a star of David on a silver chain, with a small note which read, "Forever, D".

I lifted it up to the horizon and kissed it. 'Forever.'

Papa put his arms around me, 'God has chosen for you well.'

'Indeed he has,' replied Mama.

His parents came to me and embraced me, saying, 'daughter do not be afraid. God is watching after all. He will be home.'

⌘

It was hard to keep my mind occupied. Ne, I still had school and chores and of course, Mama helped me with wedding plans. Plans that I could not become concrete until Dionysios came home. It would be almost three months before I would see him again, and about that long before I received any news from him.

Papa would hug me and say, 'patience my daughter. He is doing his duty, the work that will make him a better man.'

Themos was the first to arrive home on leave. Papa was right when he said that the army would make Nikos a better man as it seemed to do that with everyone who went into service.

His coming home made Mama's eyes dance. Her family was complete again, she would say and I started to think about what it would be like when and if I had sons and they too would go into service after being with me for 18 years. Then I heard Papa's voice which had said many times before to me, 'daughter do not put the cart before the donkey, live one second, one minute as it was the one that counted the most.'

In the morning, Nikos would rise, put on his uniform, have breakfast as he always did before going into the army and then spend the day mostly in Papa's shop or at one of his friends' homes.

Mama beckoned me to sit beside her, 'You must make things for your home. I know you will have a strong home with love, but you also must make the home full of beauty, other than yourself.' She let out a small chuckle.

I looked at her, 'thank you Mama. But I think you and Papa know that beauty comes from within.'

She looked at me with wet eyes, 'Ne, but it is also nice to have some beauty on the outside or it will be a very long marriage. Agreed?'

Remembering Dionysios' broad shoulders, his strong face and his smile, I nodded. 'Ne, it was nice to have those things too.'

'Then let us start making some doilies for the furniture.'

I had known Mama to sit at her chair for hours on end crocheting the doilies to sale and gifts, but never had I imagined that it would be me doing the same thing.

The days waiting were harder than I could possibly have imagined. I wrote in my journals and made a calendar so I could keep track of the days passing and what was coming. Having this allowed me to look forward with thanks giving of days no longer to live. As I grew older though, I now wish I would have held on to each minute of the day and lived it with gusto. Foolish? Maybe, but youth is many times wasted on the future and never living in the present.

Hours not spent with Mama or Papa, were spent over at Dionysios' home, working with his parents on the things they felt were important to fill a new home. And partially I believe, so I would spend time getting to know them. Their house was different, oh so different from ours. First of all, it's a house. Ne. The large wrought iron gates greet you and then a large wood door with a lion head for a door knocker. As you enter the foyer, it is large, so large that it still takes my breath away thinking about it. There were so many different rooms which seem to go on forever. The one that surprised me the most was the dining room which has a large carpet on the wall, which they called a tapestry. I don't know, it looks too nice for the floor but odd on a wall.

What thrilled my eyes the most was the chandelier which had so many tear drop crystals, it almost hurt my eyes. How could one clean that? And when the candles were lit, is sparkled and the light danced on the walls as if a party was taking place.

We had balconies, but not like this – these ran the whole width of the house! And inside the house not just on the outside. And the staircase, the windows, the curtains, ne, its grand, but it didn't feel like a home. Not to hurt anyone's feelings, and I would never tell Mama or them, but I enjoy the closeness that my family had in our small apartment above Papa's shop.

And the servants doing most of household chores, I could not do that! I mean, it would be wonderful not to wash dishes or clothes but then I wouldn't know what to do. Mama had always told me, 'daughter, feeling the earth under your fingernails is knowing you have done a day's work.'

As the days passed, waiting almost became a habit. My hands were never idle, but my heart kept looking at the calendar. I told that to Mama once and she said, 'then I know your love is true, which I never doubted, but now you know it's true also.'

On the third Tuesday of September, Papa sat me down and told me there was news that I longed to hear. 'Dionysios is coming home on leave.'

It had been well over three months since he had left and I couldn't believe what I was hearing. 'But, Papa, how has this gotten to your ears before mine?'

'Daughter, I talk to those on the dock. They are very aware of what is happening in the world.'

'So, I can rely on this news to be true?'

'As true as it can be.'

I sat back, 'it will be a short leave won't it?'

'The same length that we are enjoying with Themos.'

The ship that was bringing Dionysios was going to be taking Themos away. The feeling around our spiti was that of joy and sorrow. Mama's heart was heavy as her son would again leave her; however, Papa reminded her that her 'new' son would be coming. 'He can never take Themos' place, but he will fill our house with joy and excitement because of the pending marriage.'

When the day finally came, the two families stood on the dock, one to say goodbye and one to welcome a loved one home. The waiting brought so much anxiety to me. Mama kept folding her handkerchief and Papa swung his kobloli beads from side to side. Themos stood proud in his uniform and I, for some odd reason felt the urge to slip my hand into his. He looked at me and smiled, 'Ohi, you are never too old to hold my hand.'

'Efharisto.'

Soon the steam could be seen in the distance and we heard a voice from behind us, 'there she is!'

Suddenly a question entered my mind, 'Why are ships called women anyway?' But, as usual, my timing for asking the question was not right, and by the time I could ask, I usually forget them.

When the throw lines were finally secured and the gang plank pushed out onto the dock, I felt my heart fall as I was now understanding Mama's of mixed feelings of emotion.

I was shaken out of my thoughts with a hand on my elbow. 'He is so handsome.' The voice of Mama sounded that of surprise and excitement. Looking up, there stood my Dionysios. More tanned than I remembered and truly handsome in his uniform. As he walked closer, I felt Mama's hand give a shove and I landed into his arms. 'You're home!'

'For a little while my love.'

Then we kissed, no more embarrassment about kissing in public, but true affection. Everyone waited until we parted, then it seemed like a flurry of hugs, kisses and even tears. The two families were united on the dock as one.

The reunion was overshadowed by the sound of the ship's horn. Turning, I saw Themos leaning into Mama and kissing her on the cheek, 'I'll be back soon.'

Her hands reached up, cupping his head. She looked into his eyes, 'I know.' The rest of the words didn't come, so Themos took her in his arms, and she began to cry. How quick life is. It takes but a second for everything to change. He shook Papa's hand as well as Dionysios' then he walked over to me, 'I hope when I come back that I will have someone like you waiting for me.'

My heart slumped. I had never thought of Themos needing anyone. For the first time I sensed that Themos was lonely with a bit of jealousy for what I had.

It seemed that it was taking longer for the ship to pull away from the dock, turn and head out of the marina to the open sea than it did to arrive. Standing at the railing until but a speck, stood Themos waving at us, goodbye.

With the ship gone, we made our way back to the upstairs apartment. Now, I do not know why we never went to Dionysios' house which was so much grander and larger than ours, it could have been that we were closer to the marina; no matter, the chatter from our upstairs balcony could be heard way into the early morning.

As the days progressed, it became apparent that Dionysios was feeling the weight of marriage and commitment. Ohi, not in a bad way, but as he said, 'Nionios, sir, you asked me a question that I said would be answered with confidence but first I would need to go out into the world and explore my options. Do you remember that question?'

My father nodded his head.

'I need to say this out loud to everyone here so that they will understand; you asked "What is your trade?" What a question, such as I have never been asked before. I would like to respond that you know that I am going to ensure that when we are married that I can bring you proper honor as a husband and provider.'

Papa looked surprised. Ne, he knew that that should be of course, but he had never had a son-in-law before and had not thought about all that it entailed.

'So, this will not be easy for anyone here, but I will not be coming home when my tour ends, but will head to Athena and stay for one month. During that time, I will either have found my trade by myself, or come back here to Zakynthos where I begin work for my father.'

I held back the tears that I was feeling. My love was not coming back to me in the quickness that I had hoped, but instead was going to stay away an additional month! I could not, at any cost say no. If I had, it would have looked like I was selfish, and ne, today hearing this for the first time and not discussing it, I was feeling selfish. I reasoned that my future husband knew what he was doing. And as I looked at my father there was nothing but full of praise on his face. Dionysios had chosen correctly.

His tour was for nineteen months; ne, he was home within the first three, but once he had left, none of us would see him again until he came back from Athena. We spent many days and nights together talking and sharing our dreams. During his leave, we went to the beach and played in the sea and laughed. My heart was so full of love for this man that it felt like it would burst if I would allow it. He seemed to know me, as I did not have to ask for much, it was whilst there without a request.

He spoke of his hopes and the love not only for me, but for the island. It was his home, our home and a place so unlike Athena that he never wanted to take us away from it. He kept telling me about the military, something that was not to his liking. Ohi, he didn't hate it, it just made him anxious to end his service so we could be married and begin a life together.

I looked up at him, at his strong face and his wonderful outlook on life. How could I have been so fortunate to come into his world? True, some of my thoughts were clouded because of love, but I saw how others looked at him or responded to him. This was a man to be proud of and one that would make a good mate as well as a good father.

His leave felt short and I had so much more to say to him, so much more time to spend with him, being with him. However, the sooner he did go back the faster he would return. He pulled my face into his hand and smiled, 'I see you are wearing my gift.'

I smiled proudly, 'It is from my beloved. He chose well.'

'Indeed I did.' Then he kissed me, 'The next time I come home, I will stay and be yours forever.'

I hugged him and whispered, 'Then please hurry home.'

⌘

The communication between us was limited, but I did receive word that after waiting those long months his commission was finally over and he was now off to Athena.

Standing on the balcony after receiving this news, I began to weep. I had thought that I was out on the balcony alone, until I heard Mama's voice, 'The wind is coming from the north, there will be rain soon.'

I tried to hide my face, and the arms of a strong woman enveloped me, 'you promised no red eyes, remember?'

'Ne, it's very hard to know that he could be here now.'

'He has taken what Papa has said to heart. That is a sign of a very good man. You will both be better for it. Now come, I have something to show you.'
Leading me over to a chest that had always sat in the corner, she knelt down and began to open it.

'Mama, why the mystery?'

'Mystery? My child, there is no mystery...just a treasure for you to now have.'

'Ti?'

'When I became engaged to your father, my mama did as I am doing now, showing you gifts from the past, handmade linens, photos, jewelry and silver for you to begin your new life. As far as I know this has been passed down for four generations, and you will be the fifth. And,' she lifted a book out of the chest, 'this is our family history, which you now will add to.'

'How come you never have shown this to me until now?'

'Timing my daughter is everything.'

Waiting was hard for me. Every day that the ferry was to arrive, I would go down and wait. The weeks passed but I knew that I needed to be strong. Dionysios said he would return, and I believed him.

While finishing his morning coffee, Papa leaned over and held my hand 'Today, Dionysios will return.' I looked up and noticed that the clock was at nine. Today's scheduled ferry arrival would in less than an half an hour.

'Are you sure?'

'What I am told, ne.'

I leaped up and hugged my father around the neck, 'I have waited so long.'

Mama wiped her hands on her apron and exclaimed, 'we know, you are like a little bird in a cage who needs to be let out.'

Looking back on this, I should have realized how hard it must have been for them to see their sons go away to the army and now their daughter to be taken away from them by marriage!

'Do I have your permission to meet the ferry?'

Papa said as the clock ticked closer to nine-thirty. 'Ne, let us all go. Mama?'

'Ohi, I will stay here and wait, parakaló, come tell me quickly what the news will be?'

I got up from the table and hugged her, 'It will only be good.' I turned then to Papa, 'Efharisto for being my father, I am blessed.'

Running down the stairs and briskly to the docks I keep saying out loud, 'What if it isn't today?' 'What if the ferry has already arrived?' 'What if Dionysios' arrival has been delayed.'

Papa kept reassuring me, 'Patience daughter. My little girl. Patience!'

When we arrived at the dock, I stopped in my tracks. We were late, the ferry indeed had already arrived! Without thinking, I started to run faster than I thought my feet could carry me. Without knowing, I almost knocked over Dionysios. He held me in his arms and kissed me and then kissed me again. 'Today I am home. I am home to stay.'

Papa stood at the dock's edge, with a tear slowly making its way down his cheek.

Slowly we walked over to him, hand in hand, 'Sir, I have announced to your daughter that I am home. Soon we will be married but first I have come to you to tell you that I have a trade. I have come with employment at the National Bank of Greece. I will be working at the big bank that was built in the downtown center, and...' he reached into his pocket and out came a small box, and handed it to Papa.

Papa slowly opened the box and brought out a ring...no two rings; one band for me and one band for Dionysios. Papa shook his hand and hugged me, then kissed both of my cheeks and in return did the same to Dionysios. 'Then it is settled. Welcome to our family.'

We did not stop talking all the way to the apartment. Mama was waiting for us leaning over the balcony, 'he is home!'

'Ella, Mama!'

Mama ran down the stairs and greeted Dionysios in an embrace, 'Welcome home. Now,' as she was leading Dionysios up the stairs, 'there is so much to plan for!'

I turned to Papa and hugged him.

'My daughter is happy, therefore I am happy.'

Hearing Mama chatter as she prepared drinks, I kept thinking to myself, what is there to prepare for? Haven't we been planning for almost two years? Let us just do it, now! What I had forgotten was tradition; tradition states that a wedding takes place at least six months to one year after the engagement.

Mama held up her glass, 'now the engagement party.'

'Yamus' was yelled by all.

Then Dionysios said, 'now the work begins'.

⌘

With both families standing side by side a big party was thrown in our honor and the engagement was official. Since my parents' house was too small, our engagement was held at Dionysios' home, as I called 'at the mansion'. Ne, as I have described before it was one of the largest houses on the island of Zakynthos. It was grand by many and therefore most of us called it a mansion. It was decorated with an array of flowers, items made of paper and people...so many friends, family, and business acquaintances that all came and kept coming presenting us with gifts of money, jewelry and their love. Ah, and Papa. He stood tall and announced that he and Mama were both so proud to have the two families join together as one.

Dionysios' father lifted his glass and said 'so be it.'

Then his mother kissed both my cheeks and presented me with a silver necklace. 'This is a circle that represents your love for my son. Ne, there is a beginning with an end, and joined together there is a clasp that brings it full circle. That will be like your marriage to our son, may many blessings be in your life.'

I could not contain myself, I threw my arms around her and thanked her for her acceptance. 'I will remember this always and will give it to our first daughter.'

She laughed, 'Let us have you married first.'

I pulled away, a bit shy. I didn't realize that I had said this other than out of love for her son and the promise of future years together.

The band played, people sang and danced and the party went on into the wee hours of the morning. I grew tired; as I had never truly had to be the center of attention before, I couldn't bow out, this time it was for me. Even though my feet hurt and my eyes grew weary, I kept looking over at my beloved, his smile and the twinkle in his eyes told me to stand next to him with pride.

As we made it back to my parents building Dionysios kissed me and then held my hand, 'in a very short period of time we won't have to stand outside any building, we will be in our own, our spiti and be one. Efharisto so much for saying yes to me and for making my life complete.'

I leaned into him, feeling my arms around his waist; 'it is I who is thankful.' I started giggling, 'Can we not be married now?'

He threw his head back and laughed, 'if it were my way, then yes, but in time. Now it is very late, or should I say early, I will see you after the sun rises.' He walked over to the door and opened it; 'kalinihta agapi mou.'

I watched him walk down the street into the moon light and felt a tear run down my cheek. Oh, it wasn't for sadness but for joy. Feeling both necklaces around my neck, one from my beloved and one from his family, and remembered what had been said to me, 'This is a circle that represents your love for my son. Ne, there is a beginning with an end, and joined together there is a clasp that brings it full circle. That will be like your marriage to our son, may many blessings be in your life.'

As I closed my eyes that night my hand rested touching the chain, 'soon, soon.'

As Mama said, there was much planning. However, I don't remember much up until the wedding. Ne, Mama helped with my dress, actually she sewed it herself! She used her talents with crocheting and completed it within weeks. I still marvel at the quality and passion she had. Dionysios' mother was also very kind. She arranged for us to have a wonderful, small wedding at St Nicholas 'on the mole;' a wonderful church, facing the square close to the marina.

After the final fitting of the dress, Mama sat me down and shook her head.

'What is it Mama?' I asked.

'Ah, child. You know that you are not marrying into your church or faith?'

'Ne, does that hurt you or Papa? You do know that Dionysios and I love each other?'

'Ne. Papa and I love you too. So I say this out of love. The service for your wedding will be that of the Greek Orthodox Church. We will attend, and stand proud for our daughter.'

'Then what is it Mama?'

'I believe you should do something for your Papa.'

'Ne, anything.'

'Intercede and allow your father to say a prayer at your wedding? I know we will not have a Chuppah.'

I laughed. 'A what?'

'A Chuppah. That is a canopy that the bride and groom stand under before they are united. It signifies that foundation of the marriage, knowing that there is

One above us and watching over us. But this church you are being married in will not have this.'

I could feel Mama's sadness. 'Isn't there anything that can be done?'

With her eyes closed, she said, 'some say that the groom's house could also be this. By entering his house, you would be declaring your independence from your parents to your husband. But there is also the matter of the breaking of the glass.'

I tried to understand what she was saying, 'I think we can do the entering of the house thing, but what is this about breaking of the glass?'

'Ne, when the groom breaks the glass, it commemorates the destruction of the temple, and celebrates the love between each other.'

This was getting harder than I thought. 'Mama, I just thought we were getting married.'

She laughed, 'daughter, I have not been strong enough when it comes to the faith of your father. Ne, it seems to some as strange traditions or customs but it is that your fathers faith is just as much as part of your life as that of Dionysios' parents.'

'Mama, the planning, the preparation nothing was ever said about these things.'

She lowered her head, 'I am very remiss; can we not go and talk to them now before it is too late?'

Word was sent to Dionysios' family to meet and discuss a matter. Mama made sure that no one except the two of us knew what was to be discussed. When both families met, Mama stood and said, 'I am not only the mother of the bride to be, but also a wife of the man who gave life to this woman we call our daughter. I believe that I have been remiss in not asking one thing that will join both these families together in a way that none other can.'

Dionysios' father stood up, 'You sound sad when you say this, tell us what it is that needs to be done.'

Mama looked over at Papa, then to me and then spoke the words that she had spoken to me. Her gentle, calm voice was pure. It was a voice of reason. Then after much discussion, it was agreed that there would be a simple change or two so as to integrate a couple of the requests from my parents; however, not to deviate too much from the Greek Orthodox wedding ceremony.

In the ceremony there would be the circling of the loved ones, each around the other - each circle makes it one; similar to a Jewish ceremony. And, mostly that Papa would read from the Jewish Bible, The Song of Songs.

Papa stood up and kissed my Mama. 'I am so blessed.'

Dionysios' father shouted, 'this calls for another drink! A celebration. Unity is certainly the strength of this family.'

Maria, his mother stood, 'and much love.'

⌘

Things were so organized for the wedding that we had forgotten about where to live! Dionysios exclaimed, 'Ah, ne, where to live. I will take care of this. It will not be ideal but it will not be permanent, this I promise.'

In a matter of minutes, arrangements were made for us to first stay in the portion of the old Venetian type mansion of Dionysios' parents that was set aside for guests.

I laughed, 'Me, live in the mansion? Dionysios', I could never dream of it. I am from a small apartment that could have fit inside the rooms we were given.'

Mama stepped forward, 'Ne, but daughter, remember it is not your spiti, this is just a stopping place. You and your husband will find a place just for the two of you.'

'I know, and Mama. It will not be for long, as it does not feel like a home, it too big. I do hope that

whatever Dionysios and I finally share it will be like what you and Papa have.'

Pushing the hair away from my face, Mama looked at me, 'Any place can be a home but only if those sharing it make it so.' Then she kissed me on the forehead.

'I will remember that.'

Dionysios put his arms around me, 'Just for a while. We, together will find a home for the two of us.'

As I closed my eyes I thought, 'that I am sure.'

⌘

I went over to the mansion the night before our wedding. Maria, Dionysios' mother, had suggested that I should begin making a place for the bride and groom to rest. So, I brought over a couple items and as we were fixing up the chambers there was a knock at the chamber door. 'Who could that be? Did you not send the servants home?'

'Ne.'

When I opened the door, there stood Mama with a handful of her best linen. 'This must be placed upon the bed before the guests arrive.'

'Why is this? They won't care what my linen on the bed looks like.'

Mama smiled. 'You will learn, my very young daughter, that when you are to be married, your guests will throw money on the bed to help you with your future. It is called a 'wedding bed'. As the night ends, there will be a blessing said over it. Would you rather have all your dowry hung in your new home for everyone to see?'

'Hung? All my linens? My clothes?'

Mama replied, 'Everything. This too can happen, so it's your choice. Hanging your linens and clothes or making the bed with new linens?'

I could not imagine this happening! 'The wedding bed sounds more what I would want.'

Both of them laughed, as they proceeded to make the bed. I think she knew already what my response would be. Seeing them together brought joy to my heart; as here was one of the wealthiest women of all of Zakynthos and my Mama, a shopkeeper's wife working together and not talking about position or wealth but showing true love for their children.

That night, a party was held downstairs. This was to be the last, except the reception after the wedding. Guests came into the bedroom and threw money on the bed, paper bills and coins. Then I heard Themos shout, 'Who has the youngest child here?'

Natasha, my older cousin, cried out, 'I have, I believe a bebe of ten months.'

Themos again shouted, 'bring the bebe to the bed. Dionysios and Anna, please sit on the bed.'

We did as we were told and then the bebe was brought in and thrown into the middle of the bed. The room was so packed with people shouting, 'a boy, you will be blessed by a boy.'

I looked at Dionysios, 'so the tradition is, then it shall be.'

He whispered gently in my ear, 'Let's let God do his work and we'll find out.'

The bebe cried and I laughed. 'Let ours be a little less loud.'

People filtered out of the room and after awhile, I was escorted home as Dionysios went with his friends to party as he said to me, 'for the very last time.'

Mama came into my room and sat on my bed. 'I will miss you in here, each night allowing me to kiss your forehead before you go to sleep.'

'And I will miss this too.' I threw my arms around her and held her tightly.

'I know I am doing the right thing, but why is it so hard to let go?'

She rocked me back and forth in her arms, 'It's a passage that we all go through. I too had the same feelings when I was about to leave my home, my family. And look, I made it through and now I have you.'

'I'm glad you did.' Pulling back I wiped my eyes, 'no red eyes, right?'

'Indeed. That was a promise you made.'

'Then that's a promise I shall keep.'

⌘

It was the day of the wedding, what words can I tell you? Mama helped me into my wedding dress and as I stepped out into the living room Papa beamed. 'You are so grown up! And Soula the dress, you have truly outdone yourself.'

I twirled and danced and giggled; 'it is truly beautiful isn't it?'

Mama looked at me; 'the dress could not show the beauty if it wasn't already there in the person wearing it.'

I went over and kissed her on both cheeks; 'I am so very proud to be your daughter.'

Papa came up next to me and said, 'we are proud to call you our daughter.'

Mama left for a minute and returned with glasses filled with liquor. Now I hadn't ever drunk before but I am told this was champagne. You may laugh at me, but not even at the party thrown for us at the mansion did I drink. But I took the glass and Papa said, 'a toast, to the love of my life. And to Soula, for standing next to me all of my days and bringing into this world three lovely children, Themos, Nikos and our lovely daughter, Anna. And to God for bringing a new member into our family whom I know will only bring joy and happiness to our Anna's life. Shalom.' And with the lifting of the glasses we all shouted 'Yamus!' and I tasted my first sip of liquor and I started coughing.

Both of my parents laughed, 'you are supposed to drink slow.'

'I was, but it tastes horrible.'

Taking the glass Mama said, 'we can't have any on the dress, now can we?'

We heard commotion coming from the stairs and turning around there stood Themos and Nikos. I couldn't believe my eyes. I was told that neither would be there for this day, and now, there stood my brothers. I ran over and hugged and kissed both of them.

Themos held my hand and said, 'sister, my you have grown into a very lovely woman; Dionysios is one lucky man.'

Nikos laughed, 'Themos, that is your sister you are talking to but, I have to agree. You have become a gem.'

I felt my whole body blush. Ne, they were my brothers, but I wasn't used to being talked to like this by anyone.

Papa said, 'you two came just in time. Did bring the carriage?'

'As instructed.' They said in unison.

I turned and looked at Papa, 'a carriage?'

'A gift from Yannis and Maria, Dionysios' parents; you are to ride in style, with me.'

'And what about Mama, Nikos and Themos?'

'Ah, your brothers have their instructions. Now, we must get going.'

Mama helped me put on the veil, looked over my makeup and the boys helped me down the stairs. This was a feat within itself. I was in shoes that I was not accustomed to wearing, I was in a long flowing dress such as I never worn before and my hair was stacked higher than the doorway – at least it felt that way having the veil on top of all of it.

Climbing into the carriage I felt like royalty. Mama and my brothers waved goodbye as Papa and I were driven off down the street.

Not only goodbyes, but loud cheers were said as we left them standing there. A worried look must have been on my face because Papa said, 'no need to worry, we'll meet them at the church, this has all been planned.'

Now, I was told that we were to have a small wedding. The rehearsals and the talk said it was all going to be small. But when we were coming around the corner toward the church, I saw a sea of people standing and my heart leapt. 'They are not all there for…'

Papa interrupted, 'ne, for you.'

My body started to tremble. 'But they all won't fit in the church, they will be disappointed.'

'Dearest daughter, that is not of your concern.'

As we went in front of the church I pulled my shoulders back; 'daxi, I'm ready.'

But the driver of the carriage didn't stop, he kept on going down the street and around the church not once but three times! I thought he had gone mad. I turned to Papa and said, 'what is happening? Am I not getting married? Is this a game?'

Papa laughed and laughed, 'Ah, I have surprised you? As with everything in life, there are traditions and this my dear is one of them.'

When the carriage had finally stopped, I noticed a red carpet had been laid down from the steps of the square to the church's entrance and on both side of the carpet were bouquets of flowers.

'Oh Papa, this is almost too much.'

The carriage driver opened the small door, Papa stepped down and was greeted by the Bishop of the church, who whispered something to Papa, then bowed, and stepped aside.

Papa then held out his hand, 'Mrs. Stamaras, may I?'

My hand trembled. 'No, but you can help Anastasia Maria Kalamaras down.'

He laughed, 'Po po po.'

Standing toward the church I saw my beloved Dionysios, his parents Maria, Yannis; my brothers Themos and Nikos and of course Mama. Slowly we walked down the carpet toward the church. Many people greeted us and said blessings to me. Once we made it to the entrance of the church I was presented to my brothers, then to my new in-laws, and then to Mama. She almost could not contain herself. Then to Dionysios.

With Papa at my one side and Dionysios on my other we walked into the church.

Once we were inside, others followed. It started filling up fast; as I had though, there was not enough room for everyone so many stayed outside to listen. I was told that the ceremony lasted well over an hour; this I do not remember, but my memory is strong on one thing. It was when Papa stood up and read in Hebrew from the Song of Songs, 2:8-10, 14, 16a; 8:6-7a and the words flowed from his mouth like they were his own.

> *'For love is as strong as death. I hear my Beloved. See how he comes leaping on the mountains, bounding over the hills. My Beloved is like a gazelle, like a young stag. See where he stands behind our wall. He looks in at the window, he peers through the lattice. My Beloved lifts up his voice, he says to me, Come then, my love, my lovely, come. My dove, hiding in the clefts of the rock, in the coverts of the cliff, show me your face, let me hear your voice; for your voice is sweet and your face is beautiful. My Beloved is mine and I am his. He said to me: Set me like a seal on your heart, for Love is strong as Death, Jealousy relentless as Sheol. The flash of it is a flash of fir, a flame of the Lord himself. Love no flood can quench, no torrents down.'*

Papa looked up at the priest and he nodded; then he placed a piece of cloth with something wrapped in it on the floor; he crossed over and kissed Dionysios on both cheeks and then me.

Dionysios lifted his leg and brought it hard down on the piece of cloth. I heard breaking of glass and then he turned to me, 'Your turn.'

I giggled and tried with all my might to do the same, and then I heard glass break too. I laughed with joy.

Papa screamed, 'Shalom.'

Yiannis screamed, 'Yamus.'

And then there was an uproar applause and shouting.

We were now husband and wife.

I was beyond happy. Here were the two men I loved and admired the most, together, and now after almost two years of waiting I had become Mrs. Anastasia Maria Stamaras.

Leaving the church, it began to rain rice; quickly we ran to the carriage and down the street but not toward the mansion. You see, the parents need to meet you at your new home, so they must get there first. Once you arrive, then the fathers invite you in to your new home, the mothers present you with the house, some gifts and then they leave. This all takes about an hour. So, what happens to the guests? They wait. They know the tradition and they are very good at waiting as they know that once the party starts it will be one of <u>the</u> events of the year. Since we are to use one of the chambers of the mansion, the guests this time can actually be invited into the rest of the house by the parents and the party can begin, not having to wait for us.

It is actually tradition to keep the guests waiting. They are thinking that 'something' is happening between the married couple when in fact, all the married couple is doing is changing their clothes and getting ready for the party. Ne, there may be something else, but it is not spoken, and I will not speak of it here, ella!

When we did come out of our chamber and onto the balcony, there was a lot of 'OPAS!' shouted.

Dionysios led me down the staircase and onto the main floor. Toasts were made, dances were danced and two families were united.

As in the church, Papa presented us with a glass wrapped in cloth. I guess he had talked to Dionysios about this before, because Dionysios kissed Papa twice, accepted the gift and placed it on the floor. Then he stood back and stepped on it...breaking the glass almost immediately we were put upon men's shoulders and the music swirled around us. Two houses, ne two religions had been united to become one.

And the food? There was more food than I can ever think about and the drink was almost as abundant as the food, if not more so.

It was around three or four in the morning when the party started winding down. Ne, our engagement party was long, but this was different. It felt like it was meant to last for days. Finally after Mama and Papa said their goodbyes as well as the Stamaras' I looked at Dionysios.

'My husband of less than eight hours, I am a bit tired.'

He smiled, 'it has been a very long day, ne?' Then he stood up and said, 'Now is the time for us to retire, efharisto for everything.'

Kisses and hugs were given as we headed up the staircase and into our chambers. Once inside Dionysios walked over to me, putting his arms around me and said, 'Mrs. Stamaras...s'agapó.' Then kissed me the hardest kiss I had ever received from him. 'Are you ready to be my wife?'

Ah, you want details? Needless to say we did not leave our room until late morning. Enjoying each other's company why leave?

Our stay in the mansion lasted just a little over two months. Something unexpected happened... I discovered that I was with a bebe (baby).

Quickly, our parents helped us find an apartment and Mama helped me set up house. No one was more surprised than myself; I thought we would have a plan, you know, get an apartment, settle in and then maybe, just maybe try to have a bebe. When I told Mama she talked to me very patiently; 'Your body is ready. Now, you must give your husband a good home, the very best you can give.' I was a bit scared. I had just gotten married, now I was with child and in a new home; when could I find time to be a wife when motherhood was right around the corner?

The bebe grew quickly, as well as my stomach! Fortunately, I wasn't ill as much as I had heard happened, but it was hard after awhile to go up the stairs to visit Mama. So, she would bring her crocheting down to Papa's shop and the three of us would talk about what having a grandchild meant to them.

Papa turned to me one day, 'I am happy for my daughter. You have made your Papa very proud.' I threw my arms around him. That is what I had always wanted to hear.

Dionysios worked hard, six days a week, sometimes eleven hours per day. Ne, the bank was only open from 8 in the morning until 1:30 but he went to work at 6 am and came home around 1:30 to go back for a couple more hours. I told Mama that I worried that he would grow old fast.

She laughed, 'My daughter, wait until you have a child, then you too will grow old. This Dionysios of yours, is a good provider, he is making sure everything is done, not lingering around hoping for any handouts. He is a very good man.'

He would come home though and help me around the house. 'You shouldn't be lifting that. Why don't you sit down and rest?'

I finally had to say something, 'Rest? It is you that work!'

He replied, 'Yes, but it is you that not only should care for yourself, but one that grows inside.'

I threw my arms around him. 'How much more can I love you?' And that was true. Having such a wonderful husband and now with a bebe coming, it made me almost burst.

As fall approached, I knew my time was near. I asked Mama to stay close and when she wasn't around, Dionysios' mother or their maid was near. I wasn't afraid for the birth as much as afraid that I would deliver it by myself. Mama used to tell me about my birth and I wondered if I would have the bebe in my own bed! And, one evening, I went into labor and I did exactly what I feared.

Dionysios tried to stay calm, but his mother had just left so it was just he and I. He looked at me, 'What do I do? How can we do this?'

I tried to calm him down as well as myself. Maybe it was easier to have him so worried so I couldn't worry about myself. As the baby came into the world, Dionysios was right there. Luckily, his mother had forgotten to tell Dionysios something and arrived just when we needed her. "po! po!" (wow) She ran over to the bed and screamed, "Nero! Tora!" (water, now!) then grabbed my arms and said, "push!" I truly thank God that she was there to help with the delivery. And, Mama was there. Yes! She had made some dinner for us and had begun to knock at the door when Dionysios opened it with a bowl of water. 'Soula! Bravo! Ella…beba (baby girl)!' With so many hands, the beba was delivered without harm; she was laid into my arms by my Mama…three generations together.

Dionysios took his mother out into the sitting room and hugged her. 'Mama, we are a family, Anna, beba and I.'

His mother quickly dispatched him to get Papa and his father. 'Ella, Ella!'

I looked at Mama, 'Nine months, I have wondered what she would look like and now I know. She looks like you.'

Mama beamed. 'Like us,' she said, 'Like us.'

Oh, what a celebration it was that day. As I tried to rest in bed, and all of the grandparents gathered around. No matter what religion or race we were, we were united by a small child.

Mama or Maria took turns taking care of the beba; this was a blessing and a problem. They seemed to forget who the real Mama was! I did breast feed her; I made sure my time with this small bundle was long and I enjoyed every minute of it. I also found that Papa closed the shop for longer hours just to be around his granddaughter. I told him, 'When she is older, I will begin to bring her to the shop.'

'And she will stay for awhile?'

'I promise.'

'That is a promise you must keep. She is the gold when others have only silver.'

I didn't realize how tired you can be looking after a small one. But as the days wore on, I grew in strength and began to take walks to the bank (of course to see Dionysios and to show off the beba) and then to Papa's shop.

When it came to being at the shop, Papa would stop whatever he was doing and hold the bundle in his arms. 'I remember when you were young. What joy you brought to our family.'

'And what peace she has brought to our families.' I added to ensure that it was understood Jewish or not, we were all going to be a family.

As with everything, the holidays passed too quickly; the whole year did. We would join Maria and Yiannis over at the mansion or they would come to Mama and Papa's apartment. We couldn't all meet at our apartment; ohi, it was too small.

One day Papa looked at me with a surprise in his voice, 'my daughter has grown up so much this past year.'

'Ne, this year has passed quickly.' The miracle of a beba is just that to me, a miracle. First they come into the world, they cry, laugh, look like Papa then Mama and then both...their first teeth, they crawl, walk and then become a person of their own. That is what

happened to my little beba. She grew fast and began walking at eleven months. Papa would always coerce her to say 'Papa'. And he would turn to me and say, 'See, I am loved the most as she has said Papa first. And Papa means grandpa to my ears.'

One evening while we were laying in bed, Dionysios began to laugh.

'Te?'

'I was thinking about the engagement party and the throwing of the child on the bed?'

'I have not even thought about that.'

'Ohi? I guess bringing to religions together to produce a child may have backfired.'

'What if we have another one?'

'Then, it will be a boy, I am sure.'

'We won't know for awhile will we?'

'Ohi. Beba here is enough for now.'

⌘

As her dedication approached, I was asked many times what we would name her. So, at dinner one night I wondered out loud, 'What shall her name be?"

Dionysios smiled, 'We could call her beba as she has been known this whole past year.'

I looked at him, 'Then that is her name. Beba.'

'Ne, Beba it is.' Then he laughed and said, 'she grows up, goes to school, she will be known as Beba.'

After much laughter and teasing, I became more serious, 'We must be careful. If we name her after my father, as tradition would have it, then if we do have a son we cannot name him the same name.'

'Ah, I think Nionios is not a good girl's name.'

'Ne, but Nina would be her given name.'

'Then, let us name her after my mama and yours? Helena Tasoula Stamaris.'

'You are certain?'

'Ne, soon she will be baptized and be given her full name.'

'Helena Tasoula Starmaris, so it is.' I looked down as she lay in my lap asleep with beautiful eyelashes curling up to the sky. A smile had formed on her face. We both knew a secret that would be shared soon. I nodded to her. Yes, I will tell him.

After putting her to bed, I made my way into our room then climbed into bed and looked over at Dionysios. What will he say? I could not hold my joy any longer; 'what would it mean to you if I were with child again?' then leaning into him I kissed his cheek quickly then rolled over and pretended to sleep. I waited, and waited and when I finally turned over, I noticed that he had fallen asleep. 'He must have not heard, or he just assumed it was to be.'

The next morning at breakfast, Dionysios smiled at me and said, 'So, we would have to call him Nionios, or Nicky for short. And if we have another child, we will need to buy a fishing boat.'

I laughed, 'you did hear me.'

'Yes, I just didn't want you to feel like you had the upper hand.' He then reached over and started kissing me and my stomach.

Our Helena started saying, 'Papa! Papa!'

He picked her up and said, 'You will always be my big little girl.'

I then realized he had slipped something into the conversation I wasn't expecting either. 'A BOAT!'

He roared with laughter 'Oh, you did hear me.'

'Can we afford that and another bebe?'

'We need to bring more food to the table, and we can also probably sell what we don't eat.' He stopped and looked out the window, 'And wouldn't it be nice to give some to our parents?'

'Ne, and maybe you could take Papa out in it?'

'Ah, so I have won you over? Ne, your father would like that very much… and,' grabbing Helena, he started bouncing her up and down on his knee, 'what about you my Helena, would you like to ride in the boat too?'

'Ohi, Papa.'

'Ohi?'

'She must be like me, the land is firmer under our feet than water.'

Dionysios laughed. 'Then the new one in your stomach has to be a boy. One each?'

'One each it shall be.'

⌘

The next day Dionysios took Helena and Papa to look for a boat. 'We don't need a big one, just big enough for four people.'

Papa looked over at Dionysios, 'Tessera (Four), Anna does not like the sea.'

'Ne. But we still need one that fits four.' Dionysios said without looking at Papa.

'Dionysios, you work at a bank and cannot count?'

'Nionios, I have you know that I am very good at counting.'

Papa stopped and looked over at Dionysios, 'Is Anna with bebe?'

'Ne.'

'Ba!'

And off they went and found a small fishing boat for four.

While they were away, I told Mama the news.

'Anna, another one so soon?'

'Mama, it must be. I cannot change it now. And Dionysios believes this one will be an aghori (a boy).'

'One can only hope.'

And hope I did. My stomach grew and grew as the days became weeks then months. The rain came stronger than normal. Not only the rain, but the wind was so strong – wild and the thunder and lightning it stayed for days. Helena ran through the house screaming, 'why does it shout so loudly!'

I grabbed her in my arms, 'to let us know that we are not the ones in control.'

The winter wasn't like others, it was almost violent. I had hoped that it would end, but it lasted for almost three months, but that did not stop my joy.

Helena was much help, and as I was beginning to slow down, she was getting faster. 'Mama, I will be your feet.' She would say as I was trying to get out of the chair or the bed. As spring approached, the bebe started kicking hard and sometimes knocked me back until the pain was almost too hard to handle. In early April, as soon as Dionysios arrived home from work, I told him, 'the time is near to have this child see the world.'

Dionysios touched my stomach, 'I am not going to be caught like last time...I must get your mother.'

I nodded my head, 'and soon.'

Within minutes Mama was looking at me, her hand held my face, 'it will come easier and probably faster this time.'

No sooner had Mama walked in, than Dionysios grabbed Helena, 'Now I go get my Mama; she didn't miss the first one and I don't want her to miss this one either.'

I couldn't answer the pain was too great; 'Oh Mama, he wants to come now.'

Mama was correct, it was a quick birth and ne, the new bebe was a babis (a baby boy)...and he came out mad. He cried without having his bottom touched! Oh, so different from Helena, so different.

Dionysios arrived just in time, and once it was announced that it was a boy, Dionysios grabbed Helena and bounced her up and down in the air, 'Ah, now I have my little fisherman.'

I think I remember smiling at Dionysios before I fell asleep, 'One each.'

I thought I heard him say, "One each it is.' He leaned into me and said, his name is to be Yiannis Nionios Stamaras.'

'Ne, but he will still be babis until he is dedicated.' My lips moved but I don't know if anyone heard me, 'one boy, one girl.'

The apartment had a flurry of activity. Mama or Maria were helping me, taking charge of babis. And of course Papa and Dionysios who were out fishing when my husband was not at the bank of course, or at Papa's shop playing with Helena. They would come home and tell me stories of their days on the water. I was filled with joy to know that my husband and father, though not friends at the beginning of our relationship, became close because of the children and the boat.

'Have you named the boat?' I asked.

Helena stopped and looked at her Papa. This I think was the first time I had not heard her speak. Then she started to laugh; 'a boat doesn't have a name.'

'Ne.' said Dionysios, 'it too can have one. Now, what shall we call it? Christos? Yiannis? Dionysios?'

Helena started giggling so much she fell on the floor, 'Ohi! Ohi! Papa's boat.'

'Then that is its name, Papa's boat.'

Many days Mama would come over and bring food for all of us. She would help me bundle the kids so I could take walks, always walking her back to Papa's shop then continue on my way to the bank to meet Dionysios. Everyone in the bank would greet us with warm expressions of joy and Helena would get to sit on her Papa's lap and he would say, 'someday you will work here too.'

⌘

Signómi...this is so apesios (awful)...

Today was like any other day, Mama and I laughed and gossiped a little about life and when we arrived at Papa's shop, and were greeted with kisses on both cheeks, he was trembling.

'Papa?'

But before he answered, he bent down and kissed both the children.

'Daughter, it is very quiet today, be cautious.'

'Papa,' I chuckled, 'Today feels like no other day. Ne, I have noticed that the wind does not blow and there is a stillness in the air, but I am only going to the bank to see Dionysios as I always do; we will be daxi.'

'Humor your papus (grandpa), parakaló. And remember daughter, S'agapó. (I love you)' He then hugged me tight, and kissed my cheeks again.

The bebis was a bit fussy, so Mama bent down and said, 'Agapi Mou); S'agapó na.'

I tried to look deep into his eyes, but all I could see was my father's love. I hugged him again and told him, 'Do not worry, I am protected.' And I lifted the chain around my neck, 'and so are my children. Ahdio ya tora (goodbye for now)' and then with Helena skipping next to the carriage we hurried down the street.

I told Helena, 'wave bye bye to yaya (grandma) and papus'.

'Ahdio yaya! Ahdio papus!' She always made it sound like a little song.

'Now let's hurry so we can come back.'

The day was planned where I would go see Dionysios at the bank then head back for lunch with the two of them as the children would nap in my old bedroom. Endaxi?

Helena skipped along greeting shop keepers and I don't know why, but we made it particularly early this morning, around 11:15.

Entering the bank Helena ran over and interrupted Dionysios as he was talking to a customer; try as I might I couldn't hold her back from seeing her Papa. He stood up and greeted us and then as he was turning to introduce us to his customer, Signómi, my heart drops when I remember this, the building started shaking violently. What I remember is that Dionysios grabbed me and threw me under his desk, he already had Helena in his arms and I kept shouting, 'Bebis! Bebis!'

I didn't know what was happening. My eyes were filled with water as I started crying. I heard screams coming from every direction. The whole building kept moving and I kept screaming, 'Bebis mu! Bebis mu!'

Dionysios somehow managed to bring Helena to me and shouted at me, 'STAY!' and then he was gone. 'Ohi! Ohi! Bebis.'

Helena was yelling, 'Mama! Mama!'

I kept her tight against my heart. But where was my other bebe? Where was my husband? What was happening to this building? Should I have listened to Papa and..?

Then Dionysios, covered with dust, started crawling toward me carrying our bebis.

All I could do was cry. 'S'agapó! S'agapó!'

The whole building shook even more violently, at least that's how it seemed. I was losing my voice and all I could do was hold on to my family, for our lives.

After what felt like an eternity, (but as we found out later it was not more than a minute), the shaking stopped.

I couldn't seem to quiet either Helena or bebis down.

Dionysios tried very calmly to say, 'an earthquake or a bomb.'

Just then the earth shook again and stopped, then shook a third time, (we now know it was around 11:24) even more violently.

'Earthquake! We must hold on to each other.'

The light fixtures and plaster were falling and crashing around us. The kids were crying, people were screaming and I just hung on to my family the best I could. I had never known such terror. Dionysios turned and pulled my head into his shoulders, 'we are here together...all of us. Whatever happens, we are together.'

The screams were everywhere. 'SIZMOS! (EARTHQUAKE!) DON'T LEAVE THE BUILDING!'

I turned and looked at Dionysios, 'Mama, Papa?!'

'We must stay until we are told it is safe.'

I buried my tears in his shirt. How safe were we? 'Dionysios, maybe this building will fall on us!'

'Ohi, if it hasn't yet, it won't.'

Helena was sobbing, 'I'm scared.'

I tried to cradle her in my arms. 'So am I, but we must be very brave especially for bebis.' I looked up and Dionysios smiled down at me.

'And me too. Stay here and let me see what I can find out.'

I grabbed his shirt, 'S'agapó.'

He kissed me and said, 'Endaxi' then slowly left us.

My thoughts ne were on my children and husband, but I knew – at least what I could see we were safe. But, what about Mama and Papa?

Just then, I heard Dionysios' voice, 'Let me have the bebis, you take Helena. Get up slowly.'

As I crawled out from under the desk, I tried to stand, but my legs were quite shaky. As I pulled myself up all I could see was confusion. The lighting fixtures that hung proudly from the ceiling had crashed to the floor, glass from the windows had shattered all over, and papers and books were thrown around the room as if a big wind storm had come through the room.

Dionysios was leading the way, 'Watch where you walk, let us switch, take bebis and I will carry Helena.'

My head was spinning, I tried very hard to do what Dionysios told me to do. Destruction was everywhere.

Someone was trying to pry open the door so Dionysios handed the bebis to me so with one arm I had Helena and the other bebis as more men started prying open the door with their bare hands. Once it was pulled open, all you could see was rubble and sunshine.

'What do we do?'

'Well, what I can tell, we need to get away from all the buildings, follow me.'

I was dazed as we walked out into the sun; what I had known of my hometown, it was no longer.

'Ella, ella!'

I was trying to hurry, but my eyes and my mind weren't believing what had happened. All the beautiful Venetian buildings were reduced to rubble. Buildings had fallen into the street onto buses, carts, street vendors wares - everything was a total loss. Chaos was everywhere; broken glass, rocks, stones, twisted metal, shutters torn from their hinges, broken dishes and even clothes scattered throughout the streets. People were running, screaming – old women were on their knees with their hands raised to the heavens crying and saying prayers. Old men were yelling, 'Yati! Yati! Yati!' (why! why! why!)

Streets didn't look familiar. There were chickens and goats running wild; 'I need to see if Mama and Papa are endaxi.'

'Ohi, we can't go there as the buildings are unstable, we must go to the marina where there are no buildings – we must find a safe place.'

'Ala (but)...'

'Anna, they might be waiting for us, we must get our family safe, endaxi?'

'Endaxi.' That is what my mouth said, but my head couldn't help but wonder if they were safe...what had happened? Was God mad at us? Why was our island in such rubble.

Not only did we need to get away from the buildings that were in shambles, but also there were fires flaring up. People cooked with bottled gas and when the earthquake happened, those kitchens turned into ovens of fire.

We slowly made it to the marina, all the time looking up and around making sure nothing would fall on us or that we didn't fall into a hole. Then turning around, looking at our Zante Town, it was nothing but shambles and on fire.

Dionysios started asking around about my parents. Fortunately, his parents had gone to Athens for business and to see relatives. Nothing. People were wandering also looking for loved ones. 'Signómi...I am looking for...' Their eyes were filled with hurt, pain and bewilderment. I guess I too had that look.

Hours passed and still no news. Dionysios took us to the boat and there he placed both Helena and Bebis down to sleep. Ne, I believe that exhaustion replaced just being tired. I sat on the edge of the pier, 'Ella.' requested Dionysios. I could not. No matter how much danger was on land, I still felt safer than in the small boat. I knew that he would watch the children, but my heart was filled with fear. Where were Mama and Papa?

Close to 6 pm, Hristos, my parents neighbor came running up to us. 'Ah, there you are!'

My heart raced, 'Any news?'

His head fell down to his chest. 'Signómi, Anna. Both Soula and Nionis are gone.'

'Gone?'

'Ne. They were in your Papa's shop and it collapsed around them.'

'OHI!' I fell to my knees.

'They were together.'

My world felt like it had ended right then. My parents, the two people that had always been there for me would be no longer. Dionysios tried to console me, but then Helena woke up. 'Mama!'

Dionysios lifted her out of the boat and into my arms, he spoke gently to me, 'you must be strong for these two now.'

'Hristos, are you sure?'

He knelt down beside me, 'Ne. I had just left your mother with her crocheting and your father with his book work. He told me that he felt that it was too calm today. I agreed, but told him that maybe it was actually a good sign. He told me that he thought not, but as he said, "sometimes I am wrong". I told him that I needed to meet my wife at San Marcos Square and left. When I reached the square, that is when the ground started shifting. It moved so violently! I held onto my wife and brought her down to our knees and clung together. Not too long ago, I made my way to our street...our building had fallen down to nothing, and your parents the same. I know that they were there and did not leave.' Then he kissed me on both cheeks. 'I loved them as if they were my own parents, you do know that?'

'Ne.'

'I will do whatever it is to help you and Dionysios out.'

'What is there to do but to give them a place of rest.' Then I started to cry, I could not hold back my sorrow. I, like so many wept that day and many days to follow. As the afternoon turned to night, the townspeople had either assembled up on the hill or down by the marina. Fires were everywhere and what you could see – all you could see was smoke, rubble and four buildings standing. St. Dionysios Cathedral, The Church of St. Nicholas 'tou Molou" (of the Quay), the main school and, the National Bank building. We had been in one of the buildings that stood!

I do not know where everything came from, but blankets, cheese, bread and water were distributed.

I asked Dionysios if we could go to our home and see if it was standing. He looked at me and said, 'Anna, look at this destruction, do you honestly believe our home will be there?'

Families climbed into boats and stayed out in the marina away from the fires. I told Dionysios that I could not, my feet must be on the ground – unstable as it was.

He understood. He pulled the boat up against the side of the pier and tied it up. He slept in the boat, while I cradled my children to sleep on the marina's hard surface, with the smell of fires and the screams from the prison sounding in the background. Ne. Because of the instability of the prison which was located in the northern part of the town, no one rescued the prisoners and all told, 217 perished. Screams were heard hour upon hour, and it is said that even today, there are times when screams can be heard in the darkness.

Early the next morning, the sound of planes were heard in the air. They planes were American that dropped supplies from the sky as there was no air field on the island. Military men parachuted out of the planes and down onto the island. Even though they couldn't speak Greek, they tried their best to communicate with us on what had happened and how they could help.

From somewhere shouts were heard, 'Look, ships are approaching!'

The British Royal Navy had heard the news and had come with bulldozers, wood, blankets, water, and various supplies to help us out. And, a couple ships from the state of Israel! Ne! Because of what the Bishop and the Mayor had done back in 1943 for the Jews of Zakynthos, the newly formed state of Israel had sent relief supplies with a message that read, 'The Jews of Zakynthos have never forgotten their Mayor and their beloved Bishop and what they did for us.'

We were moved out of the downtown area and away from the devastation. It was a total of four days that the chaos continued. Uncertainty filled the air. The smoke rolled out from the town to the sea. Rumors were heard that some villagers from the north part of the island helped fuel the fires, but I never heard if this was confirmed or not.

It was hard to have patience when not even the bare necessities were being taken care of. Ne, tents were being set up that had simple cots, latrines and cooking areas were assembled. But, it was hot and not a lot of shade was found.

We had some news that said that the earthquake was the highest tremor recorded at 7.3 and that the epicenter was directly under the southern tip of Kephalonia. About 2/3 of Kephalonia was destroyed. Leveled. They said that more than 600 people died and with the injured and homeless, numbers were into the thousands. Between the destruction of these two islands the people were in panic. Since there was no work, no news and a feeling of total loss, many people were rumored to have left the island; 'what is left us rubble and no place to call home?'

Finally men were allowed to go to the areas of town where their homes were and check out the damage and to see if anything could be salvaged. Because I was a woman and with children, I was not allowed, nor any of the women – just in case another tremor occurred. Hristos was going to go with Dionysios, upon my insistence. Before Dionysios left, I asked him, 'Could you…'

And before I could finish, he wiped the tears off my cheeks, 'I will.'

Hristos' wife wrapped her arms around my waist, 'they will return, unharmed, God willing.'

The waiting was hard, but when I finally saw Dionysios walking up the hill, my heart leaped, he had come back to me, alive.

'And?'

'Total devastation. The island has only lost about 300 lives; it could have been worse. We might be able to get something out of our spiti, but my parents mansion, your parents…'

I looked away, I knew what he was going to say.

'I am told that the plan is to get the fires under control and then, to bulldoze down the ruins, all of it into the sea.'

'Out to sea?'

'They are planning now to make a larger marina.'

'They are going to build on the ruins of Zakynthos?'

'Ne. Even though they will build on the ruins, we will never to forget what has happened here.'

'Is there nothing to spare? Are all the Venetian architecture the mansions…our past?'

'Anna, as you know there are only three buildings that remain intact, ohi, four. The two churches, the school and the National Bank. All that the Venetians did to make Zakynthos Town so grand has been wiped out. The mansions of the rich, the Venetian architecture since the late 1400's gone forever.'

'But what about the…'

Dionysios took me in his arms, 'We will look as long and hard as we can for your parents.'

'Promise?'

'I promise.'

My body fell into his. Never had I ever thought that this would ever be happening, both of my parents. The two people most cherished, were now gone.

The island was in chaos and it felt like it could not be repaired. Slowly, some wooden buildings were constructed. As boats approached, more and more people started taking what they could and began leaving the island. Many of the rich had lost their homes, but *could rebuild. Boats that brought supplies were leaving with people. 'I have family in America I am leaving as I cannot wait for our government to do anything.' Some went to Israel, others to San Francisco, Chicago, even Toronto, Canada. Others like us were at the mercy of the state. But even then, Greece itself was going through a rebuilding from the occupation from the Second World War, and with famine and almost total destruction of its infrastructure and the four years of bloody civil war...in the short period between 1943 to 1953; those ten years over 2 ½ million people died of war and famine...the country itself was in a chaotic state, and now this!. The state itself was low on money and the money received from the Marshall Plan was used to get the nation back on its feet. We were given 25,000 drakma to help rebuild, but for what we had, that was almost nothing. Dionysios parents were not allowed to return from Athens for some time, and he kept saying, 'They are safe, and what could they do but be part of the problem now.'*

The same was true for Themos and Nikos. I did not know if they knew anything of our parents, the true horror of what had happened, but because of the shipments, at least the newspapers from Athens helped us know what news was being told to our families off the island as well as to the rest of the world.

I asked Dionysios what we should do. 'I have no one here except you, Helena and bebis. I need your wisdom now.'

He looked at me, 'The bank will not open for awhile. There is no business. I could see if they need labor to help build, we could go to Galaro and build a spiti, of what your Papa started....'

'Papa's dream land.'

'Ne?'

'Or?'

'We could leave as others have and go to America.'

I shook my head, 'if transportation can be found, I would like to go to Galaro, then, we'll see.'

I needed to be away from the destruction. There was no guarantee that there wouldn't be destruction there, but I needed to feel close to Papa, Mama, both of them.

The next day, it was arranged to go to Papa's property. The ride was long, but once outside the town, we noticed that there wasn't as much destruction. True, there wasn't much building either, oh a few homes here and there, but for the most part the land was still for farming. When we got the land, there stood the small building that for the past few years Dionysios had helped Papa build during our quick visits.

'Anna...' he reached over and touched my arm.

'It doesn't look like the city does it??'

'Ohi, but you don't know what the insides looks like.'

'There's only one way to find out.'

Dionysios helped Helena down and she began to run around chasing butterflies, then I handed bebis to him and then he helped me climb down.

'Go ahead.' He walked away cradling bebis.

I pulled the key from under the stone by the rose bush, stopped, bent down and smelled the roses. 'Mama, they are blooming beautifully, bravo.'

I went up to the door, unlocking it; I walked through the rooms. It appeared that there was only slight damage. This was our three room spiti...the living room that would serve for the kitchen and dining area, and the two bedrooms. I leaned against the wall and tears flowed. 'Papa, po. po.'

I went over to the cupboard Papa had built into the wall, 'oh, Papa.' I slowly opened it, hearing the hinges creak as I pulled it back. There inside was a photo of Mama and Papa on their wedding day. I picked it up and held it next to my cheek. I then took off the necklace with the Star of David that Dionysios had given me. Memories flooded back to me, turning it over I read, Forever. D." Taking the star of David off the chain, I kissed it and put it onto the nail in the corner. As I was placing the star, I heard my Papa's voice from my wedding…'**For love is as strong as death. I hear my Beloved.**' I just started to cry…'Forever, Papa. Mama. Forever my love will always be that strong for both you and Mama… always and I will tell the stories to the children'.

I didn't hear my husband who had come up next to me and put his neck onto my shoulder.

'It is still theirs…the memories, the…'

'I know, let us go back to our tent with the others before dusk. We will find a new home.'

The trip was filled with Helena chatting about the wonderful time she had with the butterflies; bebis slept on my lap and the roses that I picked from Mama's bush lay wrapped in the shawl that Mama had left at the spiti during one of our visits.

⌘

⌘ Helena ⌘

With the doorbell and telephone ringing at the same time, I decided to answer the door; there was a machine to pickup when I couldn't answer the phone. Reason enough I suppose, but then that was my specialty.

'My lord, Marjorie, what on earth are you doing on my doorstep?'

'Well, I thought I'd stop by and see how everything is going.' She briskly walked by and into the kitchen, 'Did I see a taxi leave here with Denny? Now, I could be wrong, you know I don't see like I used to.'

'No, you're...'

'Well, I don't mean to be a busy body, those people I just hate. Remember the Bewitched television show? It was Mrs. Cravitz wasn't it who always butted in. I hope I'm not like that.'

'Actually...'

'Good, oh, coffee smells great, mind if we share a cup?'

'I, um, sure, just made a fresh pot.'

'Well, it must be awful quiet around here with...I can mention her name can't I?'

'Nana?'

'Good. Dear woman, always greeted the world with a bright smile no matter what was going on in her world.'

I poured two cups, but before I could set them down,

'Oh, you do have cream, the real stuff don't you? Don't mean to be a bother, but having coffee without all the fixin's just doesn't settle right with me.'

Turning to the refrigerator I took a deep sigh, and started counting, She's going to say something right about now.

'You are getting the cream aren't you? Wouldn't want to drink this any colder than it is.'

Finding the cream left over from the gathering for Nana, I turned to Marjorie, 'Would you...'

'Oh, I'll take it straight from the carton, no need to make special allowances for me. You've probably had to do that for the people that were over here for Nana's...um...'

'Memorial service gathering...'

'Yes, if that's what you are calling it. By the way, someone tried to park in my driveway and I had to tell them, I'm afraid you just can't park there...what happens if I have an emergency. You never know when an emergency can happen, why, look at you.'

'Yes, well...'

'Must have been quite a scare, lands, and she, well, was up in her room?'

'Yes, she died in her room.'

'Well, I keep trying to tell people, it's actually passing over, but if you want to call it...'

'Marjorie, how's the coffee?'

'Fine. But, you didn't give me something to stir it with.'

'Oh, I must have spaced out on that...'

'That is so understandable. Thank you dear, now let's get right down to it. What are you doing to do with this old house? I mean really, it's just you and Denny and well, seeing her leave in a cab the other day, I just knew you'd be all alone and well, you shouldn't be in this big old house all by yourself. Well, that's what I was telling myself when I saw the cab drive away as I was taking out the trash. Wasn't that Denny that I saw drive away?'

'Yes, it was.'

'Lands, I knew I was right. Now, what about the house?'

'What, or who if anyone gave you the idea that I would want to leave this house? It has been the family home for well, thirty odd years.'

'I know, but it's so big and with the dwindling of your occupancy, and of course I would not want to lose you as a neighbor, you have been so dear. Do you remember the time I lost my kitty cat and your husband, what was his name?'

'Bill. William.'

'Oh, what a lovely man, too bad about that accident.'

'Marjorie.'

'I hit a nerve, I'm sorry. It's just that this house should be used again by a lovely family, just like yours used to be. Oh, dear me, I've overstayed my welcome. Here, this is what I came for, my card.'

She laid it down so hard I thought the counter would shake.

'I see it has your photo on it too.'

'They always tell you in real estate school, first impressions, are the lasting calling card. Look, I do have to run, but if you are thinking about listing, call little ole' Marjorie first, okay.'

She took another sip of the coffee, 'That's mighty fine brewed coffee you have there. I might have to come visit you more often. Lands.' And then she was off, well, not quite, she kept stopping, nodding and pointing and then when she reached the front door she turned, 'You could get a good price.'

I truly tried to get a word in edgewise but it seemed that once I tried to open my mouth she knew it and started talking first.

I reached for the door handle and she said, 'You won't forget, will you?'

'No, I won't. We really should...'

And out the door she went, 'Nice chatting with you, and that was really good coffee!'

Down the sidewalk and across the street she went. I quickly closed the door, but not until I looked over and noticed that she was, well, how do I describe it, using both of her hands and measuring the house, or trying to figure out what angle would look good on the for sale poster. I leaned up against the door and started to laugh. I laughed so hard, I started having coughing fits. Now, I'm almost sixty-four years old and I've seen nearly everything, but that woman...she did not need any coffee at all, she was so wound up. But then I stopped and looked around. The staircase that led to the bedrooms, the long foyer that was great for parties so people could mingle from the front door to either the dining room or to the living room, all of it was now silent.

What was I going to do?

Well, the first thing was clean up the god damn coffee mess left over from Marjorie.

After putting the cups in the dishwasher I picked up her card. That face, who did her makeup and her hair? Phyllis Diller and Marjorie must be sisters. I took it and threw it right in the trash; if I do sell, I won't be using her – I know there will be words, and I heard myself saying out loud, "and you probably won't get any in edgewise."

But with a dish rag in hand, I kept moving it back and forth over the counter, what do I do? 'Hey Nana, got any plans? Denny's gone off to the old country and it's just little old me in this big house. Feel like, I don't know, livin' it up!'

Then I threw the dish rag into the sink, 'hell that will be the day.'

Just then I remembered the phone call that I should have answered and pushed the button, 'You have one new message, first message. Helena, it's your uncle Nic. I'm just sitting here thinking about you and how you are holding up. Could you call me?'

Without hesitation, the phone was out of the cradle and numbers were dialed. Within two rings I heard, 'What took you so long?'

'Ah, a crazy neighbor.'

'How's my little Helena...'

'Nic...it's just you and me tonight.'

'What, where's Denny?'

'Well, Nana sent her on a little adventure.'

The laughter from the other end was infectious. 'That sister of mine, she would.'

'Say, what are you doing right now?'

'Well, at 78 not very much.'

'Good, I need an afternoon with my uncle, if that's okay with you?'

'I couldn't think of anything better to do.'

I pushed myself away from the counter, grabbed my coat, purse and keys, and out the door I went. And true to form, Nic was sitting waiting for me.

As I approached his door he yelled, 'It's open, and you're invited in.'

He wouldn't even let me set down my things, 'get over here and give me some sugar. My, you could stand to get out more often.'

'That's why I'm here, now are you ready?'

'You just got here.'

'And such a lovely place, but...'

'I love to give you a hard time, help this old man up,

hand me the good cane and let's get the hell out of here.'

I would like to say, within minutes, but it took about ten, he was buckled up in the passenger seat and I was behind the steering wheel.

'Say, how about if we agree right here, I'm moving in with you.'

I was thrown off balance, I thought it would take everything I had to get him to agree. 'Do I have any say in this?'

'Not if you have your way.' And he started laughing again. 'God it feels good to be alive.'

And off we went. No matter what you say about 78 year old men and even those you've known all your life, most of them still have a lot of piss and vinegar in them at least those from my part of the family.

Once in the house, Nic looked up at the staircase, 'How in the hell did she do it all those years?'

Closing the door and moving around him I said, "'Cause she wanted to be independent and as you know nothing stopped her.'

'There is a hell of lot of steps.'

'You don't have to climb them, we can always put you up down here.'

'Hell you will. If my sister, God rest her soul climbed them up until right before she died, then, so will I.'

And we did. Slowly. Once we got to the top and down the hallway to Nana's room, Nic stopped. 'Helen, look at all these photos; I haven't seen some of these in years. Look, oh, there's mom and dad...and Themos...Nana and...' he chuckled, 'little pudgy me.' He just stood there looking at it. 'You are born, you live, you die.' His speech got softer, 'I sure do miss them all. They were a wonderful family. I'm proud to be part of them.' Then it was like a new fire was lit under him, 'Take me to sis' room, can't wait to bother her with some of my snoring.'

As we walked I tried to inform him that there was the situation of where he was living now; 'If you call that living, then hell must be a playground.'

'I didn't know things were that bad.'

'Never knew it myself until now.'

Making it over to Nana's overstuffed chair, 'let me sit here awhile; there, well, she had a pretty nice set up here. Where's the can?'

'The bathroom is right through that door, we had one put in when we remodeled what twenty years ago?'

'Has it been that long?'

'Well, Nana actually moved in right after Bill, died.'

He reached over and touched my arm, 'We've all lost ones that meant a lot to us. The pain and memory never go away. You have me for awhile so let me make it tough on you so you will wish my time was sooner than later.'

'Nic! I only said something about Bill because that is when Nana came to live with us.' Then it hit me, Bill died which brought Nana to us, then Nana dies which is bringing Nic to us. 'Don't, not for awhile.'

'You all right?'

'Yep. Just thinking, you said you needed to use the can as you called it?'

'I sure could use the powder room if you don't mind.'

'Powder room...now who ever came up with these names...can, powder room...'

'Back home we used to call it a banio.'

'Then, Mr., off to the banio you go.'

As he went into the bathroom I held myself close; 'thank you Nana...I asked for your plans...I see you still have it in you.'

Gathering some linens from the hall closet I stopped again to look at the photo that Nic had looked at, quite a family indeed.

The bed hadn't been covered since Nana died, so I also took some Lysol spray; 'How's everything in there?'

A head popped out the door, 'real nice banio, the toilet even flushes.'

'Nic, what a time we are going to have.' I made my way to the edge of the bed nearest the chair that he was sitting in; 'Now, are you sure this is what you want?'

'Ah, made it. There's something you have to learn in life, and I thought you learned the lesson before this. Once a decision is made, you never discuss it again. It's done, teliono.'

'Here comes the Greek.'

'It's always been there, I don't use it too much because people think I'm going senile. Oh, the old man's using those funny words again. Katalaveno?'

'Katalaveno, understood.'

'Bravo. Now, finish the bed so I can take a nap, these bones can only take so much excitement.'

Within minutes the bed was made, I fluffed the pillows, Uncle Nic was snuggled under the blankets and after kissing him on both cheeks I left the room. Closing the door his voice, faint but still strong, said, 'efharisto, s'agapó.'

'Parakaló, s'agapó.'

It did feel good speaking the language of my ancestors; if he's around I better bone up on it.

Looking down at my watch I realized that I hadn't heard from Denny and maybe I should tell her that we have a new boarder. Nope, Marjorie, I don't think we'll be selling anytime soon.

I decided to use my bedroom phone so as to not be too far from Uncle Nic; it's the just-in-cases that always seem to cause the problems. It's 2:30 pm here so it's…4:30 am there, I should wait. This time stuff, I hope I got it right. I just sat there. I feel more alive than I have in recent days. Why didn't I think about having Nic live with us earlier? Yes, it would probably had been a lot, but hell, Nana and Nic could have shared what time they both had left together. Helen, was it an option though? Cut it out, you can't second guess life, didn't Nic just say 'once a decision is made, you never discuss it again. It's done, teliono.' Smacking my hands on my pant legs I shook the desire to worry, what are you going to do? Well, can't do a lot while he's sleeping. Then this brilliant idea came into my head;

okay, so brilliant it wasn't but it was the best thing other than getting Uncle Nic today; I'm going into climb in the attic and get some of the old stuff that he might enjoy looking through. And, so off I went.

Once opening the door, I realized that I hadn't really been in the attic for a while. The last person up here I believe was Denny and that was to get her suitcases. Flicking on the light and climbing the stairs, I felt like I was going to find buried treasures, well, you kinda do don't you? Things like holiday decorations are stored up here, but things that you've grown tired of, or want to 'keep for a rainy day' are up here just begging to be found again.

To my surprise it was pretty organized; Helen, you are more organized than you thought, but there is also more than you thought. Pulling over a chair to sit, I started thinking, 'Maybe Marjorie would like to help organize a garage sale...no, an estate sale they do better and they grab people's attention more. Same junk different name.' Then I started to laugh, 'Oh, you'd better invite her to at least have a preview or else she'd be on your back asking all kinds of questions. I could see it now, I'd be in the middle of a sale and there she'd be, 'Now I don't want to bother, course I don't think it's a bother just to ask a question, but really just a small question out of curiosity...but...' and it wouldn't end, would it? Maybe a sale wouldn't be the best way to handle all this stuff.

After finding Denny's old school clothes, why we never got rid of them in the first place I have no idea, now they're 'retro' and I probably could get a good price; the first dishes Bill and I had and of course some of his stuff, the shaving kit, his high school year book, no definitely not getting rid of this stuff. I found boxes and boxes that were delivered after Dad died and Nana moved over here.
Without knowing it, I was on the floor looking at photos, letters and what appeared to be legal documents.

I don't know how long I had been up there, but a voice from the bottom of the stairs startled me, 'Is that another house up there? Your secret retreat from me?'

'Um, don't come up, I'm going to be right down. I've got lots to show you.'

'Fine, I was only teasing; mind if I make my way to the kitchen for some juice?'

'Even better, I'll be there in a bit.'

'Daxi.'

'What? Is there a taxi? Nic?'

But silence. He's 78, Helen...you're lucky he even gets around like he does. The stairs! I jumped up, grabbed what I could and made my way down the stairs.

He was just getting off the landing when I made it to the top. 'Is there a fire? Why are you in such a hurry?'

Should I tell him that I am worried about him climbing the stairs? 'I think I found something interesting and wanted to show you.'

'Then hurry it up and get down here so we can share in it together.'

By the time I made it into the kitchen Nic was standing by a barstool. 'I don't think I'll manage these, a bit high.'

Carrying everything over to the kitchen table I said, 'here you can sit and look out over the backyard. I'll get us both some juice. All I think I have is orange is that okay with you?'

'Sure, it's juice isn't it. Not that powdered stuff that tastes like crap, I know that they made it for space flight, but hell, I'm not in space and prefer the real stuff.'

While getting the glasses and juice Uncle Nic was looking through what I had brought down, 'I didn't think you could read Greek. Even mine's a bit rusty.'

'No, once we came to America it was we will become Americans. You will study hard, learn the language and be proud that you are Americans.'

'Silly bitch. Signómi. I didn't mean to call my sister a bitch, but her thoughts were like so many; America is the land of opportunity, reap in her bounty and forget your homeland. I never forgot Zante, or Athena; if it wasn't for the earthquake we would all still be there living on the island that is so green and rich with life.'

Bringing the glasses over to him, I slowly sat down and reached for his hand, 'Uncle Nic, things are as they are. If we would have stayed, I probably wouldn't have met Bill and had Denny. Of course there would have been another Bill and another Denny, but again things are the way they are for a reason.'

'I have never told anyone, no one what I am about to tell you, daxi?'

'Ah, that's what you were say...'

'What?'

'Nothing. Daxi.'

His hands were strong, wrinkled with time but strong as you can imagine. There was pain in his hands and after taking several deep breaths, 'Remember I was young during this time too?'

I didn't want to interrupt so I just shook my head, yes.

'I had just told Papa that I was going to get married to a girl in Laganas. Ah, she was beautiful, Sophia. Sophia. I haven't said that name in years. In Greece, not like America and this is something America should do, all young men go and serve the motherland for nineteen months. Then when you are done, you might have a skill, you've grown up a bit and you have some money in the bank. Daxi? Being a young man is very hard because the pressure is on you to not be single, you must be married, show that you have a strong family and that they will grow in numbers. There was this girl...'

'Sophia?'

'Ne, Sophia. Themos was seeing someone in Athena, your Mama was married to Dionysios, such a good man was Dionysios. He was from a wealthy family, but he never took their money or their name to better himself. Ne, they lived in the family mansion for awhile, but why? Because Papa's apartment was too small to add another person to it. But, as soon as Dionysios had the money, he went out and found an apartment and made a home for himself and Anna. Oh, they were so in love. Anna had found the love that Mama and Papa had shared for all those years. Signómi, I digress. I was envious of this love. Being the youngest of the family I believed that everyone forgot about me, which was good, ne? I mean, Anna would have a second bebe, you, and Themos were becoming big shots in Athena so, what if Nikos didn't fit yet. So, I would take my afternoons and time off and go and hike the ruins of the island, explore the mountains, and many times go to the beach. The beaches of Laganas were beautiful. The more time I spent there, the more I learned about the sea. You see in August the carretta sea turtles come to Zakynthos to lay their eggs. I would help others to make sure that the eggs would not fall prey to nature.'

He took a sip of his orange juice, 'This is good. I'm not keeping you from your work?'

'This is exactly where I should be. Please go on.'

'That is when I met this young woman. She lived with her family there in a modest house, working the land, her family raised olives and lived by the sea. Ah, to live by the sea! Now Laganas today, I understand is a tourist trap, but back then, it was small houses and lots of beaches. Now, no one knew what I was doing; Papa always thought 'Nikos, he'll be home by supper,' which I always was. The more time I spent down at the sea, the more times I saw this beautiful girl. She was not shy at all, she came right up to me and said, 'You are not from this part of the island, why are you here, to get brown?' I laughed, as I never thought about a tan; I just loved the sea and I told her so. 'Do you own this part of the island? The sea? Or can people from Zante Town come down here and enjoy it too?' That made her mad and she left. And, at first I didn't care; I thought she was too much of herself. But when she walked away I noticed that she snuck a look back. I tried to hide but then I saw a smile come across both of our faces. I kept going back, week after week, and the more I went down there, the harder it was to get home before supper. I had fallen in love with Sophia and the sea.'

'Don't stop, do you want some more juice?'

'Ohi. I...it's just that I play this over and over in my mind. I have not told anyone this ever. I guess I believed if I did, I would lose Sophia forever. But, she is gone, is she not?'

'Ohi, she is still in your heart, just like Bill. Memories like theirs are something no one can take away from you. Ever.'

He patted my hand.

'Please, for me, go on.'

'As time went on, the bond we had grew stronger, much stronger than I ever knew could be between two people. One day, I didn't make it back from Laganas before dinner and Mama started getting worried. Papa said that I was old enough not to always be home for dinner, but when I didn't come home that night they both worried. Ne, it was wrong of me, but I finally had the love that they had. I told Sophia it was wrong to keep going on, so the next day when I arrived home I walked into Papa's shop, you couldn't go upstairs to the apartment without going through the shop and I said, 'Papa, I am in love and I want to be married.'

Papa didn't say a word at first, he continued with his papers and then as I was leaving to go up stairs he said, 'Nikos, you are very special to both Mama and myself. She stayed up waiting for you; she thought something dreadful had happened to you; now go and apologize. And this marriage you want to have, you first need to show respect to your parents then we will discuss it.' A bit of anger grew inside me. Respect? How for the past twenty-two years had I not shown them respect? Then I looked over at him and said, and I remember this as if he was sitting right over there, 'Papa? S'agapó.' He looked up, laying his glasses down and smiled. As I walked over to him, he stood up and kissed both of my cheeks, 'S'agapó. yos, S'agapó.' I loved him, I don't think there was anyone in town that didn't respect him. After leaving his embrace, I said, 'now Mama.' He sat back down and went back to work without another word. Walking up those stairs was like one of the hardest things I ever had to do. I made my parents angry with me, worried about me, something I never had done to them before. As I entered the apartment Mama jumped up and cried out, 'My bebe is home safe!' And that was it; other than offering me something to eat, there never was a question of where I was or what I was doing. So after that, I always came home for supper and made plans for Sophia to meet my family. Themos was coming back from Athena soon; it was all arranged.'

I noticed tears swell up in his eyes, his voice began to tremble, 'Sophia came into town a day early. She was staying with her aunt not more than a couple blocks from my parents apartment, I did not know this as I had headed down to Laganas to go get Sophia in the early morning. It was around 11:20 the ground started shaking and the sea started making horrible waves. I searched everywhere for Sophia, but once I found her home, her parents told me that she had gone to Zante Town to stay with her aunt for a day or two. 'I must go back to Zante Town.' They begged me not to come back because of the earth shaking. Just then the tremor started again, harder and everyone ran out into the street screaming. I fell to my knees, 'why God, why this?' The roads, what roads they were, were a mess. I walked all the way back which took me hours; once I arrived the town was in flames. I helped with the rescue crew as best as I could. Soon people found me and told me of my parents, but no news of Anna, the children or Sophia. So I continued on, night and day until finally I found Anna, Dionysios and the children and we cried and cried, the grief of losing your family, the ones who love you so much. I never did find Sophia, and when Anna asked what happened to her, I told her that I believed she must have an education first and asked her to wait until she was done. And I made up other stories that she had found a new love, things like that. After many weeks of searching and clearing debris I finally made it back down to Laganas and found her parents. They were grief stricken, she too had perished in the earthquake. If it wasn't for me wanting to have her meet my parents, she would have still been alive...' His voice trailed off.

 I sat there. What could I say knowing that Uncle Nic never married and now knowing why.

 'I'm getting tired.'

 'Then, let's have you lie down on the sofa.'

'Now, those stairs...'

'Those stairs can wait until later, there's a small blanket and you can just rest for a bit.'

The little bit was four hours. And during that time, I tried to get a hold of Denny as well as sort through some of the stuff I had found in the attic. I hadn't realized how much stuff I had brought down until a voice from behind me said, 'I take a short snooze and the house becomes like a tornado!'

Leaning back I looked around, 'so it has. I just never knew how much stuff I had of mom and dad's and well, even yours Uncle Nic.'

Pulling himself up from the couch he carefully walked over to the table. 'Yep, it looks like all Greek to me.'
Without knowing, I took an envelope and hit him with it, 'Oh, I'm sorry.'

'Normal reaction, and well, let's face it, it all Greek isn't it?'

'I'm afraid so. We left when I was so young, I never really got to learn how to read it...oh I know that o with a line through it means f, that sort of thing, but I haven't a clue how to make heads or tails of this.'

'Well, maybe that's why I'm here. By the way did you get a hold of Denny?'

'No, I left a message, these time zones and special country codes, I swear even though I'm a teacher, there are some things I could take a lesson on.'

And there was, a lot of papers, documents, photographs, seals of all sorts and just a lot of stuff. What was overwhelming me was bringing delight to Uncle Nic. 'You don't know what you have here, do you? Why, it's like a vault of documents, land documents, why this one,' he lifted up a large brownish legal style pamphlet with string around it, 'appears to be the paperwork to the spiti in Galaro.'

'The spiti?'

'Ne, mom and dad's place in Galaro.'

'Well, do they...we still own it, I mean we haven't been back in ages.'

Without even more than a movement of a wrist the pamphlet was open and he started reading. 'Mind you, I'm a bit rusty, but, um, they paid cash for the property so unless there's a lot of back owed taxes or utilities, then I don't see why this property wouldn't still be in the family.'

'Mom never talked about it.'

'Well, she wouldn't now would she; it wasn't hers, mine or Themos' it was our parents'. True, we probably inherited it when they died, but that was in

1953. And, look at this, this is a photograph of Papa in front of his shop; he worked so hard every day. Helen, you've never looked through this stuff before?'

'To be honest, no. Oh, Nana and I would talk about 'someday going through it' but that someday never came until, well, now. Nana was writing a book and she would say, 'when you're ready we'll need to bring some of that stuff down from the attic...' stopping herself, she noticed the twinkle in his eyes, 'you know there's more where this came from.'

'Let's get through this first, but if there's more, you never know what's hiding up there. Like an old Greek lottery ticket or something.'

'I could be so lucky. Okay, how do you want to organize?'

And throughout that day and the following ones, the kitchen became piles of papers, envelopes, extra boxes and photographs. Nic stayed in the kitchen and the stairs were almost all but forgotten. His spark for living increased and he kept asking for 'a new yellow pad' or 'any more of those cookies' or 'how's your next trip coming along?' It wasn't until the phone rang that I had even given a thought to the outside world.

'Mom?'

'Denny, what time is it there? Oh wait, its 10 hours ahead, so it's 9 am.'

'Wow, this is so exciting. I'm talking to you the next day.'

'Mom. Why are so cheery, it's 11 pm there.'

'Well, I don't know what news you have, but boy do I have a lot to tell you. First, Uncle Nic and I...'

'Wait, Uncle Nic is there?'

'Yes, he and I have been going through some stuff from the attic.'

'What stuff?'

'Oh, your father, your grandfather...it seems so strange.'

'You seem pretty scattered.'

'Sorry dear, are you all right? You did make it didn't you?'

'Yeah, but now I'm more worried about you.'

'Don't be; Nic and I have just had the times of our lives; we've have found old letters, some drachma, documents just a load of stuff, things I haven't even thought about. In fact, I imagine some of this is your grandmother's that she just put away.'

'How did this all start?'

'Well, actually, do you remember Marjorie from next door?'

'Nosy neighbor Marjorie?'

'That's the one, well she kinda set me on this path. Look dear, now you are all right? Nothing I shouldn't worry about?'

'No, seems to me that I should be worried about you.'

'Don't be. With Uncle Nic here, I feel like I've started a treasure hunt.'

'Good, well, I'm stepping out to have some breakfast, we'll talk tonight?'

'Sure. Be safe. Oh, has anything interesting happen yet?'

'I'm not sure, let me sort this out and I'll tell you later. Oh, I did read Nana's manuscript and her diaries or the starting of it.'

'And...'

'I wished I would have spent more time with her.'

'Me too. Okay, this is costing us both, talk to you tonight. Oh dear, s'agapó.'

'Saga..?'

'It means I Love...'

'I know what it means, but I didn't know you knew Greek.'

'There are more hidden treasures to me than you know. Night.'

After hanging up I began to realize the both of us need to learn this language if we're going to get through all this. With the receiver in its place I turned to see Nic at the table again. 'Haven't we poured over this stuff enough for awhile?'

'Yes, but what you've brought down is very interesting. If what I'm reading is correct, Dionysios' parent's owned the building that your Grandfathers shop was in, but I'm not quite sure.'

Feeling a bit uneasy, I slid into the chair next to him, 'and?'

'I believe they deeded the building to them on the marriage of Anna and Dionysios."

'So, for Nana's wedding, her in-laws gave Nana's parents the building, free and clear?'

'That's what it looks like.'

'I wonder if they knew.'

'If they did, no one ever talked about it.'

'So, the building that they were killed in...'

'Which began nothing more than rubble...what about the property underneath?'

'This needs to be reviewed, but I think that if they owned the building, they owned the property too.'

'But Nic we're talking 1953; surely someone has built over it, probably even taken possession of the property.'

'We need to have an attorney look this over, but it looks like you may own something that's worth something.'

'I know this sounds like a crazy idea, but...'

'We should go to Zakynthos.'

'You agree?'

'Why shouldn't we?'

'We. That means two people, you'd go back with me?'

'Look, I may be 78, but what else do I need to do with my time? With the nest egg that I've put away it shouldn't be a problem financially.'

'And with some that I've set aside.'

'No, let this be my treat. You're seeing an old man through airports, onto planes and the like, the least I could do is pay for it. Good, no argument, it's settled, we just need to get the plans in place and off we go. Oh, we shouldn't tell Denny either, it should be a surprise.'

'Nic, she'll know there's something up when we don't answer the phone.'

'You could tell her that you and I are going somewhere and that the only way you can be reached is on the cell phone.'

'Sounds like you've done this a time or two.'

'No, but I've been dreaming about something like this, and I can't think of a better time than now.'

Looking at him, I couldn't believe he was serious, 'Okay, I'll call your bluff; we'll need passports, airline tickets, hotel reservations...'

'Call my bluff all you want. I'll call yours, since 9/11 I've had my passport. It's locked up in a safety deposit box at the bank. What they are good for ten years so I've got at least another year left on it, and you?'

'You are full of surprises aren't you? When Denny was thinking about going to India last year she insisted that I get a passport along with her, so bluff called.'

'Looks like we're going to Greece.'

I jumped up and hugged him, 'Watch out, here comes Shirley Valentine!'

'Whatever in the hell that means.'

It's amazing what a few changes in one's life can do. Bringing Uncle Nic into my home after losing Nana was heaven sent, his spark for life, his unfailing way of staying on task and just him. Yes, the kitchen looked like a tornado, and yes, well we hadn't gotten too far away from the kitchen since he arrived but in so many ways, I was accomplishing more than I had in ages. I shake my head and keep thinking, 'all this was above my head throughout these years and I never knew.'

I finally cleared a place at the table for us to eat and when I looked over I saw that Nic had taken a seat near the patio and was looking out. 'A penny for your thoughts.'

Patting the ottoman he said, 'oh, it's going to take more than a penny.'

The invitation to sit down next to him was received loud and clear, 'Right, Mister, spill.' As I sat down I noticed that the season had begun to change once again, that the trees, flowerbeds; the embarrassment I felt at just looking at the flowerbeds but then my attention turned back to Uncle Nic. Even though we never really talked about it, I could see that his good years were behind him.

'I cannot tell you what a blessing this has been. I was actually thinking that I was going to just die, be left alone and die. The last days of my life would be the memories of everything I have lived without getting to share it with anyone. Sure, I have my friends but they too are leaving, another service another 'I'm sorry' and then we go on. When sis died, it felt right, felt like that was the time; Lord knows what that time really is and where you really go. When I was young, Papa used to sit us all in church and say, 'quiet, God's listening'.

Looking over I wanted to ask. 'Do you hear God listening now?' But I couldn't, I followed his eyes as he looked out the window.

'Now, you probably know that we went to the Greek Orthodox Church but Papa was always Jewish. I never got to ask him how he did it, but he would go with Mama every Sunday and make sure we listened to the words from the priest. He would say, 'a man of God is a servant; we all must be; no matter what path you take, always make sure it is straight to the one who lives in your heart.' We would sit, Themos, Papa, Anna, Mama and me like that, in a row. I would sneak my hand into Mama's, lean up against her shoulder, her smelling of rose fragrance. She in turn would lean into me and whisper, 'you are a good son, my heart is captured by your love.' At night she would come and sing to us or read stories and sometimes both. Papa would be down in the shop working all the time, but you always knew he was near. And before he would go to bed, he would creep into our rooms, smooth our hair or pull the covers into place and kiss us goodnight. I don't think he knew how many times I wouldn't go to sleep until he kissed my forehead. Oh, I'd pretend that I would be asleep. Even when we got older, even as men, sleeping in our beds he would still come in and be our Papa.' His head lifted a little, turning to one side, could he feel his father's kiss? Then with a small smile, closing his eyes, he sighed, 'I so much wanted to be like Papa, to be a Papa...but, well...'

So we sat there, in silence for a very long time. He in his thoughts of what was and what may have been and me, feeling something that I had missed for a long time, a fathers love.

The next morning I noticed the door to Nana's...Nic's room was closed, it was around 9 so I tapped, 'Nic?' There was no sound, I slowly opened the door and peered in; the bed had been slept in, so I went over and touched the sheets, cold. 'Nic?' I looked into the bathroom, nothing. My heart started to pound; what if? I turned to leave the room and there he stood in the doorway with a cup of coffee in his hand, 'There's a fresh pot on, were you going to sleep all day?'

'I...'

'I know, I pushed you too hard yesterday, I'm sorry. I'll try not to do that today. Now...' and he passed me and over to the chair. 'Need to set this coffee down before I spill it.' He turned, 'what's the plan of the day?'

How is this man so peppy when we stayed up so late? How was it that I slept in, one who always 'woke up before the rooster crowed' as Denny used to say and he looks like he's going to take a big bite out of life. I was a bit caught off guard and before I could speak, he had already sipped his coffee and begun planning; 'first, I think you need to start with a fresh cup of Joe; it's pretty good if I may say so myself. Had the darnest time trying to find where you placed the grounds, you keep them in the refrigerator, I've heard people doing that, but I also have heard that people put that cling free wrap in the freezer, silliest things I've ever heard of.'

Then he looked up, 'oh, you do too don't you?'

'Guilty. And to be honest, it works.'

'Never needed to use it; the best thing to cover plates and such is a good old fashioned shower cap.'

That came from nowhere, to which I fell back on the bed, 'shower caps?'

'Sure, they already have the elastic band so they're easier to fit around things. I'm so glad I moved in here, there's a lot we need to sort out.'

'Wait a minute. I'm still trying to figure out where <u>you</u> get these shower caps from. It's not like you go out and travel around a lot.'

'No, that's true. But, ask your friends, 'hey while you are on vacation, bring back some shower caps for me.' They're free in the hotel rooms and nobody really uses them, they just go to waste. And well, they feel silly just bringing back the shower caps, so they normally bring back a whole baggie which includes small bottles of shampoo too. And the big thing these days is the talk about recycling, I've been doing this for years, once you've used the caps, you just rinse them out and let them dry out. They are the handiest things; you'll see. You'll wonder why you never thought about this before.'

'Well, now, thanks for the lesson, I'll remember that. First the cup of Joe, looks like I'm going to need it.'

⌘

⌘ Spiros ⌘

'Ne, I have tria tours today and I'm already late.'

The day had started off okay, the sun was rising over the mountain and I had gone through the day's itinerary twice to know that I would be going in opposite directions most of the day; this was a good day. Tourism this year had been a bit slow and I needed to make all the money for the year in these five months. My expenses were not a lot; I helped out the family a bit, saved a bit and well, as a young man, spent a bit.

Presently, I don't have plans on leaving the home of my family, but when you have three generations in one spiti, as you probably can guess, it gets crowded, but in Greece, families live together until you are married and then what you do is build on top of your parents' home.

You see we all live at the hotel where yaya's parents had once had a home, they saw that tourism was coming and in the late sixties and early seventies they started building this hotel. Humble at first, and mostly it was rooms to sublet. Nobody came to the island as tourist unless they really wanted to come. Mostly, they went to Mykonos or Santorini. Zakynthos was, let us say, off the map. Ne, there was Corfu – ah, that tourist board knew what to do. They were allowed to put in a casino and bingo, and tourists came! True they were also closer to Venice so the ferries could carry people from Italy to Corfu for some 'fun' and then return. But Zante, until the book Captain Corelli's Mandolin became famous, no one knew of the six other islands in the Ionian chain.

True, we didn't really have anything for tourist to come to. The airport, if you could call it that, was a landing strip built to bring supplies in right after the '53 earthquake, and now it is being remodeled as a more modern welcoming beacon. We have the carretta carretta turtles, but they were ours, one of the only islands in the whole Mediterranean Sea where they came to lay their eggs and feel protected and until recently we dropped the ball a bit; as we knew they were an item that would draw people, we had forgotten how fragile and precious they truly are. And of course our history, that is what I do, is to tell our history. No one should ever forget where they are from, because as yaya states, 'if you forget your history, you forget your soul.' But there is one thing we have, no matter who you are, that everyone wants – sunshine. Ohi, we do not own it, but the Gods have shown favor for us to have the beaches and the accommodations for people to come sit by the sea and drink wine and enjoy the sun – ilios, Greek ilios, the best.

'Ahdio yaya, I will be back later.'

'Ahdiho Sprio.'

She is yelling from the laundry room, probably because she thinks she has to clean even though we have enough people to do that.

I ride from Laganas to Zante Town in about ten minutes, if there are no speed traps, farmers with their very slow tractors or many tourists. I wear my helmet because Mama rules. Not that I don't want to, but to hear her say it, 'if it's the law, it's the law!'

Arriving at the bus stop, I park my bike and hop on the bus, 'Yasus Paul.'

'Yasus, Spiros.'

'We are very busy today, mostly Germans and English couples and groups.'

'How many?'

'Three trips, Yaya says that we should be home for supper though.'

'She always does.'

'Ah, here comes the first group now.'

Throughout the morning we toured various spots on the island – The Argasi Bridge, Sarakina House and the Venetian Castle, and over to a small taverna in Porto Zoro.

'Now that we have all settled, and before you take your glass of wine, I have a story to tell you; in Greece we have many mythological figures, one of them is Zeus. It is said that Zeus went to a farm house and knocked on the door. An old farmer and his elderly wife both answered the door. Zeus said that he was hungry, 'did they have any provisions?' 'Ne, all we have though is olives, cheese and bread.' 'That will satisfy my hunger, efharisto.' Once he was finished, he said, 'I would like to grant you one wish, what shall it be?' 'We are old, we want for nothing.' 'One wish, there must be something.' 'Ne, since we are old, we wish to die together.' 'That wish shall be granted.' They were joyful, and Zeus went on his way. Joyful, because they had a promise from one of the gods! They would, when they died, would be buried together. You shake your heads and ask, 'how can this be? He is just a mythological figure? I tell you this, you will see them together at the courtyard in the center of the city of Exo Hora, the memory of them, two grape vines together, wrapped around each other, twisted upward. Zeus fulfilled his promise and even more so...they still bear fruit for others to enjoy. And now, as we say in Greece,' lifting my glass, 'Yamus!'

Paul leaned over to me, 'you tell that so well.'

'Because in some small way, maybe I believe it,' and I clicked my glass to his. What I have discovered being a tour guide is that you must believe what you tell. And so much of our history on Zante is handed down from generation to generation, I truly believe what I have been told and feel so blessed to be able to tell it to others.

After the third group had been dropped off at their respective hotels, I noticed a single woman left, I was eager to go home as it was nearing nap time, but I just couldn't leave her there, 'Where will you go?'

'Oh, you are referring to me?'

'There is no one else on this bus except Paul the driver, myself, and you.'

'I got lost in my thoughts, I suppose back to the hotel.'

'I tell you something, you are a pretty lady, why not let me take you back on my motorcycle.'

She looked at me with a stare on her face, I had to recover her immediately, 'No, no...I am not trying to pick you up, I already have a girlfriend, what I meant to say is that since this is a large bus and it's quite a drive for only one passenger, would it be all right if I took you back on my motorcycle?'

Her stare remained, 'I have never ridden one.'

'Ah, that is why you...right, and I thought you were...'

'But, I could always try.'

'Paul, you can deliver the bus?' And off we went; I tried to make small conversation with her, but she didn't seem to understand; was my English that bad? I had gone to an additional school to learn English, things you do not learn in a Greek school.

Just then the bus stopped, 'right, we're here.'

She moved from her seat and out of the bus. Paul tugged at my arm, 'what are you going to do with her?'

'Take her to her hotel, and that's all.'

'Catch up with you tomorrow. Can't wait for the details.'

'I don't think there will be any, but oh well.'

After explaining the rights and wrongs to riding the bike I told her, 'Look, we'll take a short ride first.' I was about to put the helmet on then realized that she didn't have one; 'you'll need this more than me, put it on and please whatever you do, hold on.'

And, after a bit of a rough start, off we went, down the main road, until I pulled over at a small taverna and said, 'Let's take a breather before I take you to your hotel.'

'I'd like that, riding isn't as easy as I suspected.'

Finding a small table I asked for two glasses of nero and two lemonades. She took off the helmet and let her hair flow down to her shoulders. 'Ah, it's pretty stuffy in one of these. You can have it back.'

'No, you must wear this.'

'Okay.' She set the helmet down between us and stretched out her hand; 'we haven't been formally introduced; I'm Denise, Denny for short.'

I took her hand, I've never had a woman extend a hand to me before, I took it and shook it; 'Well, you already know that I'm Spiros.'

And then she sat down, pushed over the helmet and threw her hands right in front of her 'Right, look I'm from the US and feel totally lost.'

'As I would if I went to America. What is it that you came to Zakynthos for?'

She pulled her back pack around, unzipped a pouch and took some lip gloss out and smoothed it over her lips, 'Well, my grandmother used to live here, at least that is what I've just learned, and I…want to go see the place.'

Just then our server brought our drinks and I passed the euro to him, 'Drink up and we'll go...do you know where this place is?'

'Yes, actually, well, I have a drawing.' She was pulling all sorts of papers out of her pouch.

'I see you are organized.'

'Not as much as I wish, I was in a bit of a hurry when I was living in the states...let's see...' and she started unfolding various shapes and sizes of papers. 'Ah, here.'

'May I?' What she handed me was what my Yaya would have drawn, a funny non detail of a map, but then I realized...'wait, the tree, I know where this tree is.'

'You do, how?'

'It's the biggest pine tree on the island.'

'Well, I certainly hit upon the right person. Say, the story of Zeus, what other stories of this place are there?'

'Do you read or speak any Greek?'

'No, not much.'

'Ah, well, I was going to suggest a couple books. Here's one that has always fascinated me, and it was written in a book by Xenopoulous, a famous writer from this island, it is called Kokkinos Bpaxos or in English The

Red Rock. This story is from the 17th or 18th century. A girl from a Venetian Noble family by the name of Forti Sandre fell in love with her first cousin. When her parents forbade her to see him again, she went up to Vrachos Cliff, took the ring off her finger and threw it in the sea. So heartbroken was she that she then threw herself off the cliff. That is why the side of the cliff is red, 'stained by her blood.'

'That is horrible, and sad.'

'What makes you interested in the stories of our island?'

'I'm a school teacher and find it fascinating when I hear stories or myths. '

'Ready for the ride, it is not far from here.' And sipping the last of the lemonade, we situated ourselves back on the bike. The ride was easier but finding the road that led to the spiti was a bit harder, but locating the tree wasn't. Of course I wasn't expecting a flag waving saying 'Over here!' 'Over here!' but once I did find the road, or should I say path as it was more like a farmer's dirt path to his fields we made our way toward the tree dodging overgrowth of thistles and weeds. Pulling up to the building I looked at it. Typical, built as a summer home, very small and not being taken care of. The shutters looked like they had frozen together with the cement exterior. The overgrowth around the exterior, even the path to the front door was hard to distinguish. Turning off the bike, I half turned to her, 'Well?'

'You think so?' She was pulling herself off the bike, throwing off the helmet she started running toward an old rose bush which was in full blossom, but had not been taken care of in years.

Her voice screamed with excitement, 'Oh my God...I think this is the rose bush she spoke of, look at all the blossoms and the smell, oh these are delicious. Nana I can see why you loved it so much, it truly is so fragrant.' She snapped off a bloom and kept smelling it as she leaped over tall grass and weeds and as she got around the corner she screamed again. I thought she had hurt herself. Running as fast as I could I met up with her as she exclaimed, 'look here, the Roman well. This is it, this is it!' She started laughing and clapping her hands together, then she ran over and hugged me, 'thank you so much, you have made what I thought would be an impossible task almost effortless.'

I didn't know what to say. It did seem though a bit odd for me to do this. I mean, it was close to the end of the day and here I was in the middle of Zante helping a woman who kept talking about her Nana and dreams.

Then she stopped, 'stupid American.'

'Te? I mean, what?'

'I come all this way, thinking I will find this and we do...then I realize something kind of important.'

'What is that?'

'I don't have a key. I have come so far and now this.'

This American does not know that we Greeks have our own way of getting things, 'Let me see this.' Walking around the spiti I came upon a small pile of rocks, knocking a few away I found a coffee can, and inside, a key. 'Let us see if this works.'

'How did you...' and the question trailed off as she followed me to the door.

I was tramping down the grass to make a better path than what was provided. I knew there should have been a step and ah, here it was. She was right behind me so eager to get in that I thought all she needs is to use her strength and she'll be able to get in; she doesn't need me. I needed to caution her, as the place probably hadn't been opened for quite awhile. 'Now, this place has not been lived in for a long time, we do not know what we will find.'

'Like?'

'Like anything, like lizards, snakes, furniture, spiders…I do not know these things.'

'Since you have the key, I'll let you go first.'

Shaking my head, my only thoughts were, 'women.'

The lock was hard to open, 'it does not like human touch,' then after moving it back and forth it clicked, and released itself. 'Daxi!'

'I think that means good?'

'Ne, the door is now open, before we enter, I must ask, are you sure this is your grandmother's house?'

'All that I have read, the rose bush, the Roman well and…' Together we said, 'the pine tree.'

'Then, let us proceed.' I pushed the door open as far as I could, letting as much light in to the very dark room, the stench was strong. 'It smells, of course not being open for so many years…' and my voice trailed off as my eyes tried to adjust to the change of light. 'Let me step back out, and let it air out.' I cleared the doorway for her to peer in.

Looking in she started assessing, 'There is furniture, ooh and look at that old style chandelier, you're right, the smell, it smells old, musty, mildewed…and every other adjective I can think of.'

I figured she wanted a few moments alone, so I went over and sat on the well.

'There you are...you're right, a good airing out will certainly help.' And she sat down next to me. Rubbing rose petals in her hand she then lifted them up to her nose, 'Nana spoke of this fragrance as being so lovely.' A tear fell from her eyes.

What do I know of her tears? I looked over the land, 'My Papous used to farm olive groves, work in the vineyards, like the ones that surround this house. It has been passed down from generation to generation and now I do some of the work myself.'

She looked up to the sky, 'it's so, clear, you know blue here, and of course, pointing to the vines, green.' Then she chuckled, 'and so rural.' But she seemed distracted. I kept saying to myself how overwhelming this must be.

I tried to assess that maybe she too would have some vines with this spiti, 'I think some of these vines, you know the property around here belong to this house.'

She kept turning around, 'maybe, I don't have anything but this map. Spiros, is it me or are we like in the center of the island?'

'Ne, almost exactly. Look over there is Zante Town, and down that direction is Laganas. Another story?'

'Please.' As she shifted her weight as she brushed up against me.

'You see where I pointed to Zante Town, well across the marina you see that small mountain, that is called Scopos Mountain. Scopos means like 'look out' or 'pirate lookout.' No one can go on that mountain as it is private land but on that mountain is a church called Skropiotissa. If you were to go there, it would be very hard; the road is very bad, almost nonexistent; you would need a four wheeled vehicle to get you where you would find, some say, the ruins of Artemis or the Goddess Artemis...Diana the goddess of hunting. If you were to go up there and look on the other side facing east there would be her temple in ruins. My yaya says that not too many people know of this and the ones that do, think it is a myth. Ah, in Greek mythology, Artemis, Diana used to wander around the green woods of Zakynthos whereas her brother Apollo used to lay the lira under bay trees and chant about the beauty of the island.'

'You like this place.'

'Very much. My mama says that her papa used to say, 'it is in your bones, the love of such a place as this. I believe that. Ne, I would like to travel, but I want to live here, have a family here.'

'I'm beginning to think you are right...I think maybe...you know, kinda personal.'

'It easier they say, you know talking to someone you do not know. I look at my mama or my yaya and see that they are contented with their lives. I used to scream at them and say why not do more? And they would say, 'but we have.' I never understood that. What, they have a hotel and they let people for five months come in and out of their lives? But then I thought about my papa and my Papous and then I thought 'ah' it's not about the hotel but about the love that all those people shared. What I see now is a lot of divorce in the world. But here on Zante, there is not a lot of divorce, in fact you do not hear of it. Where in the world I have read that in some places it's 50%; does that make people happy to love and then find another? It is tempting in the summer to find what is called summer love, but for me, I too must be content until that right person comes into my heart and captures it.'

The chirping of the birds and the breeze blew as we sat there waiting. Waiting for what? I do not know.

'I think I know what you mean. Where I am from, we all are going so fast that we don't stop and well, do things like sit on a Roman well. Well, we don't have Roman wells in San Francisco, but if we did, we probably wouldn't.'

I had to laugh, 'Yaya tells me every day. See the sea? It will be there every day of your life, but don't forget to stop and look at it, talk to it and take time with it.'

'You know, most young people would not listen to their grandmothers.'

'You don't know my Yaya. If I did not listen to her, she would take the broom handle and hit me with it.' We laughed together. 'Ready to go see what this spiti wants to tell you?' I reached out and held her hand, 'better than going back to the hotel?'

'Much, I would have rented a car and tried to find this place myself, then probably gotten lost.' She stopped and looked at me, 'Much.'

Once inside I tried to move a table from the window, unlatched the window and pulled it; 'this place...' but I could say no more because my concentration was on finding the shutter latch in almost pitch black, but once found the screeching of the iron created goose bumps on my arms but then thud, it fell open and the sun poured in. 'Better, now...' and I turned around to a mess. The furniture was old and looked like it had mold with a lot of cob webs. Now if yaya were here she would say how beautiful they are, but to me, they are just nasty. Denny was standing in the door way, 'it's all right, I think if there were snakes or such they would have been scared by that sound or we would have had a welcoming party.'

'Are you sure there won't be any?'

I had to chuckle. 'Okay the island has snakes. It is said that one of the founders of Zante freed the island of snakes, which I know isn't true, but there aren't that many and well, they wouldn't be hiding in a house waiting for us, now would they?'

'I suppose not.'

'But, we might meet a gecko or two.'

'Those aren't harmful are they?'

'Ohi. In fact, they eat all the bugs and become very good friends.'

'That's good.' As she slowly made her way into the room, 'it's really small.'

'Ne, most houses in Greece are, aren't houses in America?'

'Well, in some places, but Americans, well, they like their space. The whole "wild west" notion, bigger is better-wide open spaces.' By then she was standing looking at the chandelier. 'This is absolutely beautiful.'

'Very old, that is probably oil.'

'Kerosene?'

'Maybe. There is no electricity here...let me see...' then I stopped, and it just came out, 'what are we doing here anyway?'

Pushing spider webs out of her hair and trying to speak with a half held breath, 'Looking for a box on a wall...I think.'

'Okay, a box on a wall...sure, we all go breaking into homes we may or not be the owners of and look for boxes on walls.'

'Sounds crazy doesn't it?'

'Well, what sounds crazy to me is that you come all the way over here from America, you a single woman, and you don't know where you are going and then when you 'think' you get there, 'where ever that is' you say 'I am looking for a box on a wall' doesn't that sound crazy to you?'

She left. She walked out through the front door. I didn't mean to hurt her feelings but I wasn't going to run after her. Well, wasn't it crazy to travel thousands of miles to find a 'box on a wall?' Why in the hell was the 'box' so important?   As I turned around I saw a

Madonna on the wall, took it down, dusted it off and thought, 'this stuff is really old' and took it out to her, out into the clean air.

'I am impressed how old all this stuff is.' Finding her sitting on the well again. 'Are you becoming friends with this well? Do you want to throw a coin in it and make a wish.'

She held onto the lip and looked up at me. 'Foolish wasn't it? You know, to think I could just storm over here and...'

'And look for a box on the wall? It is kind of weird. I haven't had too many tourists like you, and I want you to know I've been doing this since I was about twelve, you know showing people the island. My dad was a tour guide and he would say, 'everyone has dreams, some come here looking for theirs to come true.' Guess I was the lucky one to find someone who may find her dream. Here, now look at this Madonna.'

She looked over and said, 'Yes, so?'

She must be over fifty years old, if not more. Do you see how she has this thin veil around her face?'

'Yes.'

'I believe she has protected this spiti.'

'Is this your way to make me find my dream?'

'Ohi. I know I have stories, but let me tell you about the Virgin Mary Icon; it is said that when pirates came ashore from the sea at Keri they would not see the town as the Icon of the Virgin Mary would protect their town. They would come ashore, look up and see nothing, then they would turn around and there behind them would be the town. You see, the icon shielded their sight from seeing the town. I believe in this Icon.' I handed it to her, 'She is trying to tell you that you will find the box.'

She took the Icon and played with its face and began to smile. 'How come someone so young can be an old soul?'

'I have part of my yaya and papus in me. And they have always believed in her,' pointing to the Icon, 'and why should they not? I like this one very much, Papa would tell this to me sometimes when I did not believe, 'A sheep herder saw a light from down by the shore. As he came closer, it wasn't really at the shore, but in a batch of thistles. There in the midst of all the thistles was the Icon of the Virgin Mary. He went to tell the town's Bishop. The Bishop said that "we must rescue Her, there is a reason she is waiting there. So, he did rescue the Icon and placed it in the church in the middle of Keri. The next day, as the herder was on the hill, he saw the light again. Going down he found the Icon back in the thistles! He went again to the Bishop and told him what he had seen. The Bishop said, 'Ohi, it is in the church.' When they both went to the church, it was gone. They went down to the thistle patch and there was the Icon. This happened several times. So the Bishop set fire to the thistle patch, but the Icon remained and without harm. The Bishop said, 'This is a sign, the church must be moved to this sight.' And it was. If you look on the back of the Icon today, you will see blackened marks where it appears to have been touched by fire.'

'You should have been a priest.'

I began to laugh, 'me a priest? I love women too much. Now, ready to go find the box?'

She patted the Icon and said, 'On some wall, somewhere...' and off we went.

And we searched, it wasn't easy looking for a box on the wall in the dark or semi dark with all sorts of debris in our way, taking pictures off the wall, opening more windows and shutters, looking in closets, cupboards. For a small spiti it was full. After what seemed like forever, Denny stood in the middle of the room, 'it's not here.'

'You said it was a box...maybe it isn't really a box?'

'Do you mean we may have been looking for something that it isn't?' she pulled her hair back and held it in place. 'Nana said...' 'Nana are you listening? 'Nana where would you have...' and she started slowly looking around the room and then she stopped, 'Spiros...' then walked to where I had taken down the Madonna, and began moving her hand over the wall. 'There seems to be...' and as she tapped the wall, it popped open. 'The Box! It was a box in the wall...'

I moved closer as she began to take out a photo of what looked like two people and then she gasped.

'Te?'

On the back of the photo was, 'The Star of David...it's here. I found it. I found it!' and then she began to laugh.

'Te?'

'The Icon of Mary guided me to the Star of David. Oh Nana, the sense of humor you have.'

⌘

⌘ Yaya ⌘

The ending to a life is so unlike the beginning to some. I do not remember the birthing canal or my first breath of life, and now at the end of my journey, I may not remember my last breath, but what a journey in between.

Signómi, this bucket I am using to mop the lobby is heavy and at my age of 72, it does not lift as easy as when I was younger. Of course, I do not lift or move like I used to.

The couch over by the window looks inviting, so let me just sit for a while. Oh, these are not weary bones, but bones that are getting tired. I looked in the mirror this morning and wondered who that person was that was looking back. So I brushed the hair off of my forehead, pulled it back into a bun and said, 'Kalimeria, signómi, do I know you?' Then I laughed and said, 'ne, somewhere inside it's me, I can't see me with all these wrinkles.'

If you cannot laugh with yourself, then when can you?

When you are young, you are told that a girl should be a beautiful, with a shapely figure and a boy should be handsome with a sculptured body and then when you grow into your twenties and thirties you will be admired and life will be 'worth living,' so you live and work and if lucky, play. Ah, and then the forties when you find your first gray hair? Did you not find your first gray hair then? I did, but with my blond hair it looked like I was allowing the sun to bleach it a bit. Then the fifties, what a hard time, I have heard so many travelers come to this hotel in their fifties and say, 'retirement is so close, but I cannot have it yet.' Retirement? In Greece we do not retire, we look at life as one adventure that should be lived until your final breath. Ne, you may, sit on a couch more, but each day is to be lived. These 'retirement people' slowly die or find another job to do. I hear that they have money to do what they have always 'dreamed' to do; tell me, do you wait until you're fifty or sixty or even seventy to start living your dreams? I do not understand why you have to wait so long to live dreams. If you dream now, you should live them now. Did you not say when you were young, 'when I grow up I...' are you not grown up and you still say, 'when I...' When, may never come.

    We now reach those wonderful years of the sixties, seventies and now eighties but I will not talk about them, as I am there now and I think you understand that if you live that long, you breathe the air in more and know that today is the only day you should enjoy, as it might be your last!

You think I'm a philosopher, ne? Ohi, just a woman who has lived her years. And if you find that you are honest with yourself, you get up, open the drapes and say 'thank God I have survived another night of dreams to see another sunrise.'

Oh, look up there, in the corner of the room, do you not see it? If you do not, maybe the guests won't either, another cobweb.

Now, that is a wonder to me, these tiny little creatures have this wonderful way about themselves. They, somehow, weave a web so beautiful...ah, I would, but I don't ask the guests to, 'look, look up there, there is another beautiful piece of nature's art. See how the sun light hits it, how it is so woven that you become fascinated with the way it is done.' Ohi, I do not think so, the guests would look up, but when they did they would say, 'this is not a clean hotel, we should not pay for such outrageous prices when it is not clean.' Clean! Just because a spider has made a work of art?

'Opa!'

I will, somehow, get that spider web down and destroy his masterpiece. If the spider lives, he can find another corner, ne, another hotel to make his artwork in. And since the guest haven't arrived yet, I still have time. I will admire the art work for another hour, ne, another day.

I have heard that some places don't have seasons; I understand this to be true such as Los Angeles, California. But, here, we do. Last year we even had a dusting of snow! I know, in all my years on Zakynthos, I might have seen snow maybe twice. We did not go out and make snow men, but it still is something to see snow fall, the way it floats through the air. When I meet God, I want to ask him why he couldn't have made rain a bit softer, like snow. He will probably tell me that 'If I had, then you would have wanted snow even softer still. Such things were designed as they are, daxi?' Ne, I will talk to God in Greek. I know that God speaks Greek, he invented it, He should have it pretty well down by now.

I will also ask him about war, famine, hunger the things that still hurt my heart this very day. When I hear someone laugh it makes my heart jump for joy, to hear of hurt and pain it makes my heart beat faster. There are so many things to discuss with him, no wonder we will have eternity to spend with him. He will have the answers, and I will have the time to ponder on those answers.

Signómi, I went from seasons to God. Seasons are what I was thinking first. Here we know when summer is coming, all the hotels and shops start opening their doors, brooms are being used and there is a sound of work. Not that there wasn't work being done any other time, but when summer begins to arrive, you can hear it. Motorcycles and cars moving here and there and trucks are delivering supplies, blocking the driveway so you cannot leave your hotel. That happened to me yesterday, ne. I had swept the front veranda and had made my way down the steps to the front gateway of the hotel. We were expecting the water delivery for the pool, ne; we have a large truck deliver the water, it is fresh and expensive. So, I am out to the front gateway and could not go any further. There was a truck sitting in my way.

I took my broom handle and tapped on the door to ask him why he had settled so easily in front of my hotel. And when I did, he started yelling at me and saying, 'Crazy old woman quit hitting my truck, you will dent it.'

Well, if I wanted to dent it, I would have really hit it harder. I was just tapping on it.

Finally, Yiannis from the taverna next door came over and said, 'What is the matter?'

I told him that the truck was blocking my entrance.

'He is delivering and won't be a just a minute.'

And I looked at Yiannis and said, 'Frankly, I don't care. I want to see outside my entrance. It is my entrance, has been my entrance for years and since I don't ever block his entrance, I didn't want mine blocked either.'

I know that Yiannis was probably thinking the same thing as the driver, 'Crazy old woman.'

But I stopped him before the thought went too far and said, 'Look, I have had this spot since the day I was born, our spiti stood where the front of the hotel stands now. So, at 72 years old I think I have the right to have my way and not have the front entrance to the hotel blocked.'

I started to walk away and then I turned, 'And, maybe I am a crazy old woman, but wait till you survive this life and stand in my shoes and then people will say the same about you. NOW MOVE THE TRUCK.'

With that I turned, walked up the steps, sat on the chair next to the front door and waited.

It moved. Now, it wasn't like I was Moses and the Red Sea had parted, but Yiannis yelled at the kid in the truck, and it moved. Then Yiannis waved his hands at me and said, 'Daxi?'

I nodded my head, 'Endaxi.' And as he walked away I yelled, "Efharisto, parakaló!'

To get things done, you have to stand on principals. Now I know that the truck would have moved sometime, but I don't want to feel taken advantage of. Oh, I know Yiannis will tell others around of what happened and have a laugh about it, and the driver will go and tell people about the 'crazy lady at the hotel down by the sea' but I can probably tell you, that if a truck drives up again, Yiannis will be out there telling the driver, 'it is not a good idea that you park there, but maybe a bit further, and I wouldn't ask why.'

Once the truck moved, I swept to the front entrance and in front of the wall, pulling weeds and feeling the breeze from the sea.

The sea. The sun beds will come out from the tavernas that face the sea, ne they charge for them, they rake the sand so that it is smooth, then they bring out the sun beds and face the sea. Some have umbrellas others not, but they do not bring out the pads to the beds. Ohi, you must go and pay for the sun bed and then you get the pad. I have never lain on a sun bed, I prefer lying on the sand with a towel.

You do not see me lying that way now. Ohi, I couldn't get up! And, can you just imagine all the young people looking at this old woman on the beach soaking up nature's wonderful rays of light. That is when they would say, 'see there is the crazy old lady; she has lost any marbles she has left, lying on the beach to get a tan.'

I would not do it to get a tan, ohi, but to feel that marvelous warmth, feel the heat warm up my bones and maybe even take a nap like I used to do when I was a young girl.

You look at me and say, 'You were young?'

Ne, I was young once. I shake my head as I think, 'when was that?' 'When?'
So long ago. So, so long ago.

Look, I had forgotten that I had put the clean cloth in my apron. Hmm, it still smells fresh. That's right, I placed it in my apron when I was getting the mop bucket filled with water. I hate to dust. You start at one end of the room, and by the time you get to the other, you need to start all over again. Dusting and using one of those machines they call vacuum cleaners? Tugging and pulling to get dirt up. We do not have a need for one of those machines here. Our floors of tile and the rugs we have are gathered up by my grandson, and hung up for the cleaning women to hit and air out.

Ne, I have cleaning women, several actually. I cannot clean all ninety rooms of this hotel, plus the banios, the kitchen, dining area, the office, hallways and reception area by myself.

There are two shifts. Two come in the early morning to prepare for the breakfast and serve from six thirty to nine but stay to clean up and start changing the rooms as the guests leave. The guests can stay until noon and if I like them, I let them stay a bit longer and of course if there isn't another reservation for the room. Do I charge extra? Ohi, if I like them. And then the other three cleaning women come in around ten to ten thirty to start cleaning rooms and the hotel. You ask why I clean, why not only them?

Even though I own the hotel, this does not mean that I just sit and watch. I have learned from my mama; she said, 'Daughter, I tell you this. Work beside not on top. Make sure they respect you, also make sure that they see you will do the same as them. That you know all jobs but you will not take away their jobs to cut corners or any drachma. That you will be there to help, to show knowledge and to share in the load but, you are still the boss.'

Do you know the drachma? Mama was not alive when the Euro changed our world. The Euro is what I say, the 'world currency,' well almost; it someday may make take over even the dollar. Why did we have to change? Because of this thing called the European Union. Everything went higher with the Euro. Something like a bottle of nero was one hundred drachma when it became the Euro it was one Euro...double the price! Now, many travelers never noticed at the beginning, but we who live here did. Everything went up overnight. It hurt many of us. I know it is easier to go from France, Germany, Italy, Spain and Greece all over Europe and never worry about the lira or drachma, it is all Euro, but then, to me you lose your identity. Ne, we still have our flag, but to this day, I still convert everything from drachma to Euro.

I do not like this Euro. Mark my words, there will be problems.

Signómi. I sometimes take a stand on my beliefs.

I have rested enough, let us dust, or at least move some dust from here...to over there; it will find its way back soon.

These tables? I do not like these tables. My daughter said that they were more inviting than the ones we used to have before we remodeled, or the couches. I do not mind the couches, but these tables, the other ones were not as dusty.

Christina my daughter, my only child has taken over managing this hotel a couple of years ago, my, almost twenty years ago. As with my mama, Christina still asks my opinion and does not do anything without consulting me. However, these tables we still disagree on; she does not dust the tables so therefore she does not understand. I have one or two of the other tables in my apartment, upstairs, facing the sea. Ne, I have a balcony that I get a clear view of the sea. Some nights, I sit up there, sipping my tea, reading a book and watch the sea.

It is hard during the summer though, the bars with their loud music and all the commotion – young people being young people; you know Laganas never was like this in the sixties, there was only beach here and a couple houses. No one ever thought about tourists or bars or loud noises.

I have always lived in Laganas, in this cove facing the sea. Papa harvested olives a bit with his brothers and when he could, bought this property, built a small spiti and moved Mama down from the hills of Macherado.

Mama loved the sea; she said, 'I will live and die by the sea.' And that she did. She never thought about traveling other than going into Zante Town and even then she did it sparsely. She would wake up, open the curtains throughout the house and warm days, all the doors and say, 'Kalimeria ilios (sun)!' 'Kalimeria thalasa! (sea)'

She enjoyed living. She busied herself with housework, cooking and of course Papa. When he would come home from a hard day in the olive groves she made sure his belly was full and a smile was on his face.

There were days when people would come from around the island down to the sea of the Laganas Gulf. Many would swim in the sea, drink at the taverna and Mama would help out serving cold drinks, some fruita or cheese and bread.

Stavros who owned the tavern shared Mama's love for the sea. He told her that there were days when he could use her help and mine too if we wanted to. She said, 'but I will not get to enjoy the sea.'

'Ohi, the sea is always there. You can stop and look at it whenever you like; while you are doing that, make some drachma too.'

'I will have to discuss this with my husband.'

'Do and you will see that he will be okay with it. You are home, with your daughter by the sea.'

That night, after I had gone to bed, I heard them talking. Papa laughed as Mama told him of the people she served and what she had made. He could see her happiness. It was he that said, 'since you are already serving food and working, get paid for it. Why don't you go to Stavros and make an agreement.'

This caught Mama off guard as I heard no noise from the cusina. She had told me earlier that, 'Papa would never go for me working; I will need to be here when he returns. I have always been here and he likes us being a family.'

I crept out of bed and closed my doors, but it wasn't silence that I started hearing, but things that you only hear in the night.

The next day there was so much commotion that it woke me up earlier than even the sun did. Papa was already fed and had left when I walked into the cusina. I was greeted with 'Kalimeria kori (daughter) ti kanete (how are you)?'

She was chirping like a bird, she asked again, 'ti kanete?'

I rubbed my eyes and all I could manage was 'kala (good)'

And then she started telling me of what had happened last night, at least most of it and what her plans were, which included me. She would rise even earlier, clean, cook and sing...ella, her singing was like a bird. Papa would watch his dove as he called her, dance and sing around the spiti. She truly enjoyed helping at the taverna and she made enough money that we could add on to our spiti, soon people started staying at our house and Mama would charge for a room and some food. It was like having a large family in our spiti.

Games were played, indoors and out, wine was drunk and olives ate and then you would hear "Yamus" and it seemed our house was full of celebration.

After the tourist season Papa set Mama down; 'is this not hard work for you and our daughter? Are you not exhausted by all you have to do? You rise early and stay up late.'

'It is a bit, but look at the money we have. And I do as Stavros told me this early spring, if you want to look at the sea, then stop and look; it will always be there.'

And so it was decided to build onto our spiti and make rooms that face the sea and not into our spiti, 'proper rooms for rent' as Papa called them, with their own banios and a little privacy. It became that way even to today. In the winter we build and change, making better – different so when the tourist came again the spiti now a growing hotel would be clean, newer and ready to rent to them. Let me tell you this has taken years, some forty, fifty years it has not happened in one season, ohi. Now if I want to sit and look at the sea, I sit, the sea has been there for me all of these years it will continue.

At the beginning, as I said people from the island would come, a lot of young men and women. They were nice to me, but ah, one of them. He was the 'bebe' of his family, so they say. But to me, he was a handsome man who had just come back from the service. Mama noticed that I liked him, so she said to me one day, 'Daughter, go and play, it is warm and it would be good for you to play with those of your own age.'

Without hesitation, I took off my apron, adjusted my hair a bit, gave Mama a kiss and ran down to the sea. Ah, the sand under foot warm and inviting. I squealed a bit, I felt free. Running to the group I said, 'How is the water?'

'Warm,' one replied.

'Come join us,' another one said.

So I did, and it was wonderful. With that, I went up to my handsome soldier and asked, 'You are not from this part of the island. Why are you here, to get brown?' And he laughed, he laughed at me. 'Do you own this part of the island? The sea? Or can people from Zante Town come down here and enjoy it too?' He was more stubborn and abrupt than I had thought, so I turned and walked away. This is not the handsome soldier that I had in my mind, but he still was handsome; he had his shirt off and was more tan than I thought so maybe it wasn't for him to get a tan, but to enjoy the sea. Perhaps I judged him too quickly, but Sophia you could not go back and say this, so I snuck another look and when I did I was surprised as he was shyly sneaking a look back at me! And I smiled, but quickly caught myself; I had been too quick to judge, then I ran; I ran as fast as my legs could carry me back up to our spiti and grabbed a towel and began cleaning tables. Mama looked over at me, said nothing and went inside, I turned kept taking small glances at the sea to watch him. Ne, I hope he comes back.

And he did, the next week he came up to the spiti and said, 'Signómi, nero?'

I didn't know it was him at that moment as I was setting the tables and my back was toward him, 'sit and I will serve you, nero only?' But when I turned around, he was pulling out a chair, sitting down and looking right at me with a broad smile, 'Signómi for last week', and then he brought his hand up, there was a rose in it, 'forgive me?'

All I could think about was, 'Nero?' and off into the cusina I went. My heart was pounding and my brain didn't know what to say, he did come back, with a rose...I didn't take the rose! Pouring the glass of nero I took a deep breath, just then Mama looked at me, 'daughter you are flushed, are you daxi?' and then she looked out and saw him, 'ah, let me.' And she took the glass out and started to talk to him and then there was laughter and when she came back I saw she had the rose; 'he's nice; he said since you didn't want the rose, I could have it, but he still prefers you to me. Now go and play in the sea...but not too long, there will be lunches to serve.' I ran over, kissed Mama and went to meet my handsome man, my officer. That is what I had always thought of him as 'my officer' and I said, 'Sir, would you like to feel the warmth of the sand under your feet instead of here with your glass of nero?'

'Ne,' he then drank all of the nero, laid down some drachma and stood up, 'come let us.' And we walked and talked and I almost forgot about the lunches. His name was Nikos. And, my dreams came true, as he was an officer.

He stayed until about four, helping wash dishes and sweeping the pergola when he said, 'signómi, I must get back to Zante Town, my Mama insists that her family be home for supper.'

Mama replied, 'but supper won't be until eight or nine.'

'Ne, but we also must be home before Papa closes his shop and takes his nap.'

Mama went over and hugged him, 'you are truly a good son.' And kissed him on both cheeks, 'so go, and Sophia, walk him to the edge of the road to make sure he starts his journey.'

I looked at Mama. This was to mean that I was to be alone with him. 'Hurry or he'll be late.'

As we walked Nikos said he couldn't be back until next week and I said, 'I will be here waiting, at this spiti by the sea.'

He got on his bicycle and rode off north on the road and away from me shouting, 'Agapi Mou!'

I watched until there was no more of him. I whispered into the wind, 'Agapi Mou.'

He came back as his promised, and all summer long he would stay for that one day and help us, this was his day of relaxation and he worked with us. Mama tried to pay him for his time but he said, 'It is payment enough when I can come and be with you two by the sea.'

One afternoon when everything was done, Mama said, 'let us close and go see Papa in the olive groves. He had started preparing a part of the land to plant vines for wine.' So we took off, Mama, Nikos and myself. Papa had not met Nikos yet so it was a bit of a startle when he saw three of us coming toward him. Now, we had not visited Papa or his workers since we had begun serving lunches at the spiti so when he saw us he yelled, 'Ya! What is this?' And as we got closer, his next question was 'who is this?' And through the afternoon, we sat under the olive branches, talking and speaking of what was. Papa kept looking over at Mama, then me and then to Nikos. He was a man of few words but as the sun was setting on the water's edge he said, 'love is one thing, but for me,' and he reached for Mama's hand, 'it is something that must last forever.'

It seemed that Nikos was taken by this, 'Ne, I agree. My parents, Nionios and Soula have been married for around twenty five years, they are from two worlds that should not have fit but do and have produced three children. We love our family and understand what family means.'

'Then,' Papa said, 'what is this with Sophia?'

'It is love.'

My heart was in my throat, Nikos had never said those words to me and I found a tear falling down onto my cheek.

'My heart is filled when I am with her and your family.'

And that was all that was said, because what else could be said? A silence had taken place and was not noticed until Mama stood up and said, 'Nikos, it is so late, you will miss supper.'

He jumped up, 'Ne, and it does not look like there will be moon light to carry me home.'

Papa said, 'stay at our spiti in one of the guest rooms, but leave early tomorrow and explain everything to your parents, if they are as good as you have mentioned, they will understand.'

And we walked together, all four, back to the spiti and the sound of the sea hitting the shore.

The next day he left very early, even before I awoke. 'Mama?'

'He is gone, go sit outside daughter.'

'Is this bad news I need to hear?'

'Ohi.'

So I sat and waited.

She brought out two cups of tea, 'now this Nikos.'

I tried to say something, but she held her hand up, 'he is a good man, kind and so in love with you. He has spoken these words and I see it in his eyes. Do you feel the same?'

'Mama, I never heard the word love until he spoke it to Papa yesterday.'

'Ah, so this was not a plan to kidnap Papa into something?'

'Kidnap? Ohi.'

'Calm my daughter. Drink some tea. Look at the sea.'

I did as I was told, the tea was warm, not strong and the sea, it was smooth and the waves slowly tumbling onto the shore with the sun reflecting off of it.

'Always remember that anything you do, you must first take a glass of tea, sit down facing the sea, allowing time for your drink and the sea to give you answers. These will always be your friends. Ne?'

'Ne.'

We sat with the rumbling of the waves giving into any conversation.

I couldn't help but ask, 'love, it is such a strong word.'

'Ne, it can also be a word that leads to many mistakes. The two people who believe that they have love, not in love, that they can share between themselves is very special. I have heard this and I believe it is true. Always ensure that your life is like a well made bed. Make sure that the sheets are clean that the spread on top is without wrinkles and that pillows bring rest to your head. I have found more than someone to love with Papa, but to share everything with – you must also know each other's souls. You too, must find that person.'

'Nikos...'

'Ah, Nikos, ne, I feel that he is a person you, my daughter can find that with.' She reached over and touched my hand, 'don't let him know any different.' She squeezed my hand and smiled.

Without saying a word, we finished our tea; holding hands. I didn't want to let go.

⌘

I have been trying to dusting with this towel. I have noticed that it is not a good one, it has stains. I must get a different one. Mama used to say, 'you must start off with a clean one at all times. What is the purpose of having a dirty towel to clean with – you cannot clean dirty with dirty. Clean linens are always important.' So, I pass that wisdom down to the staff every chance I have. Some, in the past have tried to turn a table cloth over or hide a stain. When I see this I say, 'guests will see that dirt, any dirt. And if they see dirt then it is dirty even just a spot!'

At the end of each summer and ne, again before we start the new summer, Christina and I go through the linens. All of them from the bed sheets to the table clothes and napkins. Ne, we still use linen napkins. Mama used to say, 'this shows that you care about your hotel and your guests'. I have another reason for using linen napkins. So I won't feel guilty about another tree being cut down just to wipe someone's face!

As we sit here, in this very room, with baskets and baskets of towels and sipping our tea, we talk and sort. Some say this is a tradition, 'you are doing what you and your Mama used to do.' I say, 'maybe, but it is work that has to be done. And, I get to share a little precious time alone with my daughter.'

I have a list of things that need to be done daily, the daily routine. However, like some, these things are not done by one person each day, but I may do it one day, the front desk person another and so on. I have had Spiros do these chores when he has said to me, 'Yaya, I am bored.' This word bored, I do not understand. How can that be part of anyone's lives? There is so much to be done. Signómi. I looked at the tables and chairs out on the veranda and noticed that they need to be cleaned. If I can find the time, I will do it today, if not, maybe when Spiros gets back from his duties as a tour guide he will help. I have noticed lifting a cloth to dust, or a broom to sweep is not as hard as a heavy bucket of nero and soap!

Ne, this must be done soon, so that there will be time for the breeze to dry them so the linens, glasses and silverware can be placed on them.

When Mama first started, and when Nikos helped, Mama would say, 'wouldn't it be something if all the tables would have crocheted table cloths on them?'

Nikos smiled, 'Ne, but you must be careful as they can get very dirty.'

Mama looked over at him, 'you are very wise, I will remember that when I get those types of table coverings.'

Signómi, my mind has wondered again. That happens sometimes, am I not right? You are thinking about your work and then something from the past arrives and takes over. Like when I want try not to eat and then something sweet enters my thoughts. I resist, sometimes, and then other times I go into the kitchen and cut a piece of cake. Then I think, 'why have I done this.' No one has seen me do this, only my mind and stomach know what has happened. Then, I feel too tired to continue what I should have been doing all along, work!

Where was I? Nikos? My mind says, yes, Nikos.

Ah, it was hard waiting the whole week to see if he would return, I had thought that after getting home early in the morning and speaking to his parents he might have changed his feelings. But that morning we heard the sound of hooves beating against the road and as we looked out there we saw this man riding a large black horse.

'Mama, it's Nikos!'

He rode up to the spiti and after stopping jumped off and ran into my arms, 'if your father permits and of course,' looking over at mama, 'your mother does too, will you marry me?'

I threw my arms around his neck and kissed him. I kissed him in front of my mama! Arm in arm we went up to Mama and after his greeting her with kisses on both cheeks he presented her with a package, 'for you.'

'Do you not mean for Sophia?'

'Ohi, these are for you, only for you.'

Her hands were shaking. It was a large package with string tied around it.

She set it down on one of the tables, knocking over two of the glasses; Nikos caught them just in time before they fell to the ground. The string dispatched and the paper spread, Mama's hands went up to her face in surprise, 'Nikos! Crocheted tablecloths.'

'Ne.'

'They have cost you a lot of drachma!'

'Ohi. They are a gift from my family to yours. My Mama makes them and sells them in Zante Town.'

She could not contain herself, reaching over she hugged and kissed him several times, then she began lifting the table cloths out of the package. 'They are so beautiful.'

'And no two are alike. I hope you do not mind.'

'I will treasure these always. Efharisto Nikos. Efharisto Soula and Nionios! Efharisto! Efharisto!'

Then he turned to me, 'I want you to meet my parents.'

'Ne, when?'

'I must get back to Zante Town for I have to do some extra work, can you arrange to come in two days?'

'Two days?' I turned to Mama, 'Signómi, Mama. Nikos asked if I could meet his parents in two days time?'

'Ba, Nikos, you brought these table clothes to charm me to say ne?'

'Ohi, I came down here to ask first, but Mama said that since you liked these items very much that I should bring them at this time.'

'It will be arranged.'

Nikos gave her kisses again and turned to me, 'in two days. I must hurry; that is why I am riding a horse, too much to do.' He held me in his arms and kissed me again, 'S'agapó.' He jumped on the horse and sped away throwing kisses as he left.

Turning back to Mama I asked, 'how can this be arranged?'

'Ah, Stavros will have a delivery tomorrow morning and I will have you ride in the trailer on the way back. You will stay at your aunties overnight, be rested to meet Nikos and his family the next day.'

'But I will be early.'

'Ne. Surprise Nikos as he surprised you.'

And that is what I did, my heart sang all day and it was hard to sleep that night. Once the delivery was made at the taverna, I rode back in the empty trailer, it was not an easy ride. Roads were not smooth but full of holes and very dusty but we got to Zante Town that afternoon and as arranged, I stayed with my auntie's that night.

The next morning as I was walking out of Auntie's building, the earth shook. Not just a little, things started falling, people started screaming and the next thing I knew I was struggling to open my eyes. Someone told me, 'lie still, you've been hurt.'

My body ached, but all I wanted to do is sleep.

⌘

'How long?'

'About three days, maybe four.'

Trying to get up I found that my body wouldn't move. 'I need to...'

'You can't move.'

I was in a make-shift hospital in a tent village, covered with bandages and my hair was all cut off. It took another week to get up, then about two more to walk and get back on my feet. The bandages took even longer; once they were removed I looked in the mirror; the young girl with the flowing black hair wasn't staring back; I didn't know who this person was. Then I started to cry, 'Ohi! Ohi!' The doctor came rushing over to me, 'you are in shock' and within minutes I was given a shot to settle my nerves. My recovery took much time; as I began to recover I started hearing bits of what had happened. I told my nurse that my parents must find out that I am alive, that my...officer too.

When word reached my parents and they came quickly. Fortunately the destruction was minimal in Laganas. After our reunion I asked about, Auntie and Nikos.

Papa had a grave look on his face. 'Auntie like you have some wounds, but is healing well, you will see her soon. But Nikos...' his voice quivered, 'His parents are gone, buried in the rubble.'

Tears filled his eyes, 'he loved them very much...he...'

Mama touched his arm, 'he was out in the fields helping his sister's husband's family when it happened. He rushed back to finally find his sister Anna, her husband and children down by the marina. Praise be to God, the bank where they were in saved their lives.'

Papa continued, 'But when he learned about his parents his face filled with grief. He is a very brave young man. His next thoughts were of you. He got to Laganas as fast as he could. I was getting things arranged to go to Zante Town to look for you, but when he arrived he said I should stay with your mother and that he would go. And, whatever the word was, he would get it back to us.'

'When he left...' Mama started to cry. 'I thought I had lost you.' She began to cry into my hands.

Papa put his arms around her. 'She is safe now.'

'And Nikos?'

He took a big breath, but continued, 'He hugged your Mama and said, she can't leave me now. Then left. I had heard that he began searching by himself, then joined a search team...daughter you will not know the town it is...gone. Fires everywhere, do you not the smell of smoke?'

'Ne. Mama, how long has this been?'

'Some three weeks.'

'I've been gone for three weeks?'

'Ne. Nikos kept looking for you...and then it was announced...' Her voice trailed off, 'that you were...dead.' She started crying, 'but you are not...' and she bent down and laid her head onto my chest, with Papa next to her, 'God of mercy saved us.'

My mind kept thinking and then without much thought, 'if you all thought I was dead...'

'Nikos couldn't bear to live here without his parents, without you...he left the island. His heart was broken.'

'But Nikos loves this island...me...' as hard as it was not to cry, I couldn't stop the tears from flowing.

Papa continued, 'He sat out on the veranda.'

Mama interrupted, 'the very table, the one where he sat when he brought you the rose?'

'And he looked out to the sea, and mumbled, 'if it wasn't for me wanting to have her meet my parents, she would have still been alive...' Then he got up, and left. We have not seen him since.'

⌘

My voice, it is trembling... Signómi. I do not shed tears of things so many years ago. Oh, so, so many years.

Signómi, that bucket of water and mop are not going to clean this floor by itself, now will it?

⌘

⌘ Spiti mu ⌘

Walking up the steps of the hotel I looked up, 'Hotel Sophia'. I had to chuckle, 'Didn't you say that there was someone you once loved who lived in Laganas and that her name was Sophia?'

'Ne. So many years ago.'

'Sit here and wait for the bags while I check in.' I left Nic by the front door to sit on the chair. After giving our names, our passports and a credit card, I couldn't help but wonder, 'Signómi, I couldn't help but notice the name of the hotel. It isn't perhaps named after anyone?'

'Ne, Miss Sophia.'

'Ah.'

'She is sitting out there on the veranda.'

'Really, do you think she would mind if we chat with her for a moment?'

'Nope, but she doesn't deal much with the affairs of the hotel.'

'It's not about that. Thank you.' I left the check in and walked over back to Nic.

It looked like I had shaken him from a nap, 'Well, that took a bit, did you get us checked in to this place?'

'Yes, I did. It is going to take a bit more time to get our things up to the room; how about we go out to the patio and have a sip of something cool and look out toward the sea?'

'That would be nice, but if it has some liquor in it that would be better.'

'Oh Uncle Nic.'

'So, lead the way.'

'You know I can't wait till Denny gets here.'

We walked past reception and out through some grand french doors; as we progressed out to the patio, I saw an elderly lady sitting with a glass in her hand, looking out to the sea. 'Signómi, do you mind if we share this patio with you?'

'Daxi.'

She smiled, and continued with her drink.

How can I do this? 'Uncle Nic why don't you sit on this side, that way I can sit close to the door, just in case they need me for anything.'

'As you wish.' Sitting down he made a remark that made me almost jump for joy, 'my Laganas has certainly changed.'

BRAVO! I just have to steer the conversation, because if this IS Sophia I won't have to do much, if it's not...well, who knows? 'Well, it should, it's been what since 1953 that you were here last?'

'As the memory serves me there was just a small spiti about here and a taverna over...no it can't be as this feels too fussy now, maybe I'm all wrong.'

I couldn't help but notice the older woman playing with her glass. I think I've just put the worm in the water and the bait is about to be taken. 'Yes, you can be wrong, doesn't the sea feel good? My, to have seen this all before the changes.'

He nodded, 'Yes, these changes do not seem to be for the better. You can't see the sea like you used to.'

Then he pointed, 'See that island? We used to swim out there and back. We're race, I usually won.'

'It doesn't look like they let you swim out there now.'

'The water is so warm, when it hits your skin you feel almost reborn.'

'Talking of water, I don't think we're going to get a waiter, server whatever they are called here, I'm going to rouse one up.' Leave now and see what happens. I leaned in and kissed his cheek, 'you'll be fine?'

'I'll be all right.'

'Won't be but a minute.'

'Take your time. The breeze feels good.' Uncle Nic closed his eyes and took a deep breath.

Slipping away, I almost felt too guilty, but I was getting thirsty so part of the excuse was a total lie.

⌘

'It isn't the same is it?'

'No, but the breeze still feels the same.'

'Mama used to say, 'Always remember that anything you do, you must first take a glass of tea, sit down facing the sea, allowing time for your drink and the sea to give you answers. These will always be your friends.' So ne, things have changed, but I still have my friends with me.' And she lifted her glass.

Nikos smiled.

'You know, I remember when I was a young girl working with my Mama at the taverna, there were these young people that came from all over the island to play in the sea.'

'I too remember coming down here to swim...' His voice trailed off.

'Never did I think anything of these kids, but Mama made sure that I went and played in the sea with them.'

'I can still feel the sea, the warmth, and laying on the sand, laughing.'

'There was this one young man, quite handsome actually who, asked for nothing but brought such joy into our lives.'

Nic slowly opened his eyes, 'and he would ride a black horse down here, and take this girl on rides from one end of the cove to the other. They would laugh, run in the sea, set tables in the taverna and plan for the future.'

'They made so many plans, with so many dreams.'

'And then life happened...' tears started streaming from his eyes.

She sat her glass down.

'I looked and looked for you.'

She put her hands in her lap and closed her eyes.

'After the earthquake...and Mama...Papa, I got down here as fast as I could. Then, when your Mama said that you had gone into town a day earlier, my legs buckled from underneath me. Your Papa pulled me up, gave me the address of your aunts and I...' His voice began to shake, 'the town was torn down. The street, your aunties street was just a couple blocks from my parents, and, the buildings.' He gasped for air, 'gone. Made into rubble and I screamed, Why? Why?' I started pulling at the blocks, the twisted door frames, the...after what seemed like hours a Red Cross team came up to me and I joined in to search...for the relief and recovery...my Mama...Papa...you...gone...' He started to weep, 'I couldn't find you... I told your parents...I couldn't find you....'

'They were told that I had died in the earthquake...and that is..."

'...what I was told. I left because losing you was...'

Sophia stood up, crossed over to Nic.

'I couldn't stay...I died with all of you.' Nic glanced up to Sophia, 'I am so sorry, I couldn't live on Zante any longer.'

'And I couldn't leave hoping you would return.' Sophia leaned into his body, bringing his head into her breast, wrapping her arms around him, 'S'agapó, Agapi Mou.'

Nikos cried like he had that day so many years earlier. But not for the pain or sadness, but for love, he had once again found his love and with a quiver in his voice he responded, 'Agapi mou....S'agapó.'

⌘

Sonnet –to Zante
Edgar Allan Poe

1837

Fair isle, that from the fairest of all flowers,
Thy gentlest of all gentle names dost take!
how many memories of what radiant hours
At sight of thee and thine at once awake!
How many scenes of what departed bliss!
How many thoughts of what entombed hopes!
How many visions of a maiden that is
No more- no more upon thy verdant slopes!
No more! alas, that magical sad sound
Transforming all! Thy charms should please no more-
Thy memory no more! Accused ground
Henceforth I hold thy flower-enameled shore,
Oh, hyacinthine isle! O purple Zante!
"Isola d'oro! Fior di Levante!"

⌘

Edgar Allen Poe lived in England from 1815-20 with family members – he is originally from the US and moved back in 1820.
(This could have been published while he worked at the Saturday Visitor [newspaper] Baltimore MD in 1837)

Acknowledgement

This book could not have been even a thought if it wasn't for a conversation that Myra Donnelley (Don's business partner) had at an arts meeting in November 2002. Bored, we started passing notes, 'what do you want to do when we sell the building?' And Don's reply was 'buy a house in Greece.' To which Myra replied, 'I think I know someone who might have one.' Next thing we both knew we were on a flight in December to Athens and then on to Zakynthos.

To Anastasia Stamaras whom we purchased our spiti from; to Carolina Stamaras Nahas and her mother Maria of the Ionios Art Hotel for many question and answer sessions over cups of Nescafe' and lemonade; for Spiros Kalamaras for being the best Greek son any man could ever want and for whoever invented the internet it has provided me endless hours of research answering questions and providing new ones and for a wonderful gift I never expected- an editor, Ken Ericksen. I wish to also thank Stacey Field, Lynne/Richard Conway, Nathan Horn and for you the reader for taking this adventure with me.

For further research on Zakynthos

www.zakynthos.gr/english/history/

www.e-zakynthos.com

http://www.zanteisland.com

Places of interest on Zakynthos

The Municipal Library, The Venetian Castle, The Monastery of Agios Dionyssios, the churches of Agios Nikoaos, Panagia Aggelon and Panagia Faneromeini; Strant Hil, Grigorios Xenopoulos House/Mueum in Zante Town.
The Monastery of Panagia Anafonitria in Anafonitria.
The ruins of the Medieval Tower, Vrysakia Aqueduct and Stone Bridges in Argassi.
The churches of Agios Nikolaos and Panagia Dakrirooussa in Vassilikos.
The Venetian Tower, the churches and the Monastery of Agios Georgios in Volimes.
The Monastery of Agios Ioannis Prodromos in Katastari.
The church of Panagia Keriotissa , the Mycenaean Domed Tomb (stone built vaulted grave) in Keri.
The churches of IPapanti, Agios Timotheos and Mavra and the village Agios Leon in Macherado.
The Monastery of Panagia Spiliotissa and the Church of Taxiarhes in Orthonies.
Stone Bridges in Alykes
Forklore Museum in Katastari and Vasilikos.
Maritime Museum in Tsilivi.
Sarakina House near Mouzaki.
Famous of them all – Navagio (shipwreck) bay.

About the Author

Donald I Horn aka Donnie is a playwright, author, director and producer [well over 150] theatrical productions. His first book, a biography entitled *Crumbs of Love (and that's all you'll ever get)* was well received, and he is currently writing a sequel entitled *Crumbs from the table of love*. He has written well over fifteen plays and four musicals including *'69 – the sexual revolution musical*. A father of two and a step father of three, he and his partner divide their time between homes in Portland Oregon; Lincoln City Oregon; Palm Springs California and Zakynthos Greece. He holds a BA and MBA from City University Seattle WA.

Made in the USA
Charleston, SC
13 September 2011